I0788436

CHOSEN AS THE BREEDER

PREGNANT WITH FOUR ALPHAS' BABIES

BOOK ONE

BELLA MOONDRAGON
OLIVIA BHELLE KILDARE

For our husbands

CONTENTS

1. Chapter 1: Three Million Dollars for…Me?! — 1
2. Chapter 2: Arriving at the Castle — 7
3. Chapter 3: Rescued by Pure Muscle — 13
4. Chapter 4: The Examination Gone Terribly Wrong — 19
5. Chapter 5: The Luna Suite — 25
6. Chapter 6: Rules of Engagement — 31
7. Chapter 7: A Friend in Need — 37
8. Chapter 8: Pieces of The Four Alphas — 43
9. Chapter 9: Screaming and Crying — 49
10. Chapter 10: Schemes — 55
11. Chapter 11: The Man Who Will Claim My Virginity — 61
12. Chapter 12: Who Will Be My First? — 67
13. Chapter 13: Kissed by an Alpha — 73
14. Chapter 14: Sleeping with Mark — 79
15. Chapter 15: A Battle at Breakfast — 85
16. Chapter 16: Waking Up — 91
17. Chapter 17: So Many Doubts — 97
18. Chapter 18: If That's the Best You Can Do — 103
19. Chapter 19: Tristan Is a Wild Man — 109
20. Chapter 20: Or Maybe He's a Jerk — 115
21. Chapter 21: Having a Ball — 121
22. Chapter 22: It is a Contest, After All — 127
23. Chapter 23: Leaving… With the Girl — 133
24. Chapter 24: The Next Alpha — 139
25. Chapter 25: Slightly Embarrassing — 147
26. Chapter 26: Eli's Rod — 153
27. Chapter 27: I'm So Stupid — 159
28. Chapter 28: Visiting the Doctor Again — 165
29. Chapter 29: Winning — 171
30. Chapter 30: It's All About Emily — 179

Mated With Four Alphas Chapter 1: Slumber Party with Tristan — 185
Also by Bella Moondragon — 191

CHAPTER 1: THREE MILLION DOLLARS FOR...ME?!

"Three million dollars is an awful lot of money for only a few months' worth of work."

Quiet voices filter into my ears from the living room, and I pause to listen, hoping that my parents are not discussing me.

Then... I hear my name, and I know that they are talking about me. Again.

"Rose is a fine young woman," my mother is saying. "Any Alpha would be happy to have her."

"I know, I know," my father agrees. "I definitely think it's worth it for us to send her."

An Alpha having me? I don't know what this is about, but at least it's not about a job.

The last time I caught my parents talking about me was right before I found out that they'd gotten me a job at the sewage treatment plant of the pack neighboring ours. Not exactly the glamorous job the daughter of an Alpha would expect. But I'd taken it and worked there for a few years to help my family with their enormous debt.

"I know that it would be the answer to all of our prayers, Karen," my father adds, before confessing, "But I'm worried she won't be able to do what they want her to do. After all, our little Rose isn't that bright. She can be a real idiot sometimes. She might not even know which hole to put it in."

My father's harsh words sting as I try to figure out what they are talking about. Do what?! I couldn't help but think about all of the times he had called me names. Idiot isn't that bad compared to some of the other things he's called me. Still... It hurts, and I realize that tears are stinging my eyes.

Why can't my parents just love me like the other kids I know who have parents that love them unconditionally?

My father, Alpha Howard, and my mother, Luna Karen, are not very good at keeping the books up to date for the pack. That's because the money isn't there. And everyone knows they've dipped their hands into the coffers to pay for projects at home.

When our natural resources began to dry up a few years ago, my parents were no longer able to hide the fact that the pack was in massive debt–and that they've been the ones spending most of the money.

So... I'd done what I could to help them, and I would do it again now if I had to. My pack means so much to me, despite how awful my parents can be, someone has to take responsibility for saving the pack.

I kept listening, pretty confident that I wouldn't get sent to a sewage treatment plant. I'd ended up getting fired for throwing up on the job too many times…. Go figure.

"This is different than last time!" My mother sounds annoyed, and even though I can't see them through the crack in the doors where I am listening, I can practically see her rolling her eyes.

"She's not going to throw up all over the Alphas!"

"You hope," my dad says, and that catches me off guard. Before I can think too much my dad continues, "But there will surely be daughters of Alphas and Betas from all over the kingdom trying to get this position. Why in the world would they ever choose Rose? She's hopeless!"

So this is about a job. I try not to frown at my father's lack of faith in me. Even though I don't even know exactly what they're talking about. Maybe he's right to feel that way. Maybe I'm not capable of doing whatever it is they are talking about.

The idea that I'm about to embark on another awful job makes my stomach twist into knots. As unbearable as it is to live with my cruel parents, at least here, I know what to expect. It's not as if I can just leave. I am the Alpha's daughter. If I left my home before I married, it would make everyone question what was going on here and destroy the pack's reputation; my parents would never allow it.

But the way they are talking at the moment makes my palms sweaty and my head feel dizzy. I wish I could've left a long time ago.

I need to know what it is before I form an opinion, but I'm too scared to move forward because I know I will be punished for eavesdropping. I adjust slightly on my feet, and the floorboards squeak, which should've let them know that I was there, but they keep talking.

Our house is so old and rundown, they don't even notice that I'm the one making the noise and not just the foundation settling–again.

"We will send her. I have no doubt she'll find a way to screw it up, but at least we will have given it a try. It's better than letting her continue to stay here and mess our lives up even more," my mother declares.

"Fine," my father agrees. "I'm just saying… don't get your hopes up. Chances are, she will fail us with this as she has with everything else she's ever been asked to do on our behalf."

I feel my heart drop into my stomach, a lump that's barely beating.

Is that really what my parents think of me?

Whatever it is they are sending me to do, it sounds terrifying. Maybe they are right and I can't do it. I do fail so frequently at whatever they ask me to do. Their standards are unreasonable. At least, that's what I tell myself.

There are other Alphas involved, so that means their standards will be just as high as my father's.

No, I can't do this. I want to run and hide! No matter what it is, it's just too terrible for someone like me to even give it a try. I need to get away from here–

I hear footsteps coming in this direction and realize I need to hide the fact that I've been eavesdropping on them. I back up several steps to the sink and turn on the tap, grabbing a glass out of the cabinet and filling it, like I'm just getting a drink of water.

"Oh, there you are, dear," my mom says, the word "dear" coming out of her lips like she had to force it. "We were hoping to speak to you. Wait—you weren't listening were you?"

I turn and look at them, taking a sip of my water before setting the glass down on the counter. "No, I wasn't listening," I lie. She seems to buy it. "What is it, Mom?" I ask curtly.

"Well, there's a job opening up at the castle. King Gene is looking for a very special young lady to fill a specific role, and we think that you would be the perfect candidate for this new job." My father smiles, like he really feels that way, even though I've just heard them both say that they think I can't handle this job either.

"What job is it?" I ask.

My parents exchange an uneasy glance, and once again, I am reminded of the sewage treatment plant.

Surely, it can't be anything that shitty.

"Well, honey," my mom says, "it's a very important job."

Why are they stalling? Why can't they just spit it out? "Yes, you said that," I remind her.

"The king is trying to decide which of the Alphas will take over his position as king, once he retires. Since he has no children, he's decided to appoint one of four Alphas to become the next Alpha King." My dad smiles, like he thinks he might get the job.

That will not be the case. "All right..." I sigh. "What does that have to do with me?"

Another uneasy exchange of glances passes between them. "The Alpha who takes over the throne will need to have an heir," my mom explains. "And... that means... they need... a Breeder."

The water I swallowed a moment ago seems to have come back up, and I find myself choking. No one asks if I'm okay or tries to comfort me as I attempt to breathe. Eventually, I recover enough to ask, "A Breeder? You want me to be a baby making machine for an alpha?"

I can hardly believe what I'm hearing. I'm a virgin! I've never even kissed a man before! I've been saving myself in hopes of finding a true love match that will become a fated mate, but from what I'm hearing, none of that matters now.

"That's right, dear," my father says. "The pay is excellent, and it would give our pack some much-needed status in the kingdom."

"But what about me?" I ask, annoyed. "You're okay with essentially selling my virginity to some random Alpha?"

"Honey, it's not like that," my mom says. "It's an honor. A lot of Alphas and Betas are sending their daughters to try for the position. We are only hoping that you'll be the best suited."

I shake my head. "No, please."

My father's hand lashes out and slaps me hard across the face. I recoil as my cheek lights on fire. I should've known better than to tell him no. This isn't the first time he's slapped me. "Don't you tell me no, little bitch!"

I step back, out of his reach. "Mom, Dad, please! You know I've always done everything you've asked me to do, but you can't seriously be asking me to do this! To sell myself to an Alpha I don't even know?"

My dad takes a deep breath through his nose. "I think you're misunderstanding a couple of things, Rose," my father says. "First of all, we're not asking you to do anything. We are telling you. You'll leave tomorrow."

"But Dad!" I begin. He holds up a hand to stop me, and I'm not sure if he might strike me if I don't stop talking. He has done so before.

"The other thing you're misunderstanding, Rose," he continues, "is that you will not be a Breeder for a random Alpha."

I take a deep breath, hoping that means I won't be a Breeder at all. "I won't?" I ask worriedly.

"No, daughter," my mother says. "There are four Alphas, and they've already been selected, so it isn't random at all!"

My spirits fall as I realize my misunderstanding had nothing to do with not having to become a Breeder. That is still the job they are giving me. It's just the random part I was apparently wrong about.

"So… I'll be assigned to one of the Alphas as a Breeder?" I ask them.

Again, my parents shake their heads. "No, that's not it at all," my father says, clearly growing agitated again.

I lean back against the kitchen counter, feeling myself grow dizzy and weak in the knees from so much discussion about such a terrifying subject. "What is it then?" I ask.

They have an internal debate about who has to answer that question, and it is my mom who draws the short stick. With a deep breath, she says, "Rose, you won't be a Breeder to one of the Alphas. You'll be a Breeder to all four."

"All four?" The words echo around in my head, but I can't absorb them. It just doesn't seem possible. My parents are willing to sell me to all four of them?

I'll have to have sex with four different men?

"No!" The word escapes my lips before I can even think about it, and once again, I feel the sharp blow of my father's hand contacting my cheek.

The stinging inside of me is worse than the smarting in my cheek, though. I can't do this....

That lightheaded feeling envelopes me, and the next thing I know, the world is turning dark at the edges, and I find myself giving way to gravity.

The last thing I hear is my mom saying, "Rose, really?" and then the world goes black.

CHAPTER 2: ARRIVING AT THE CASTLE

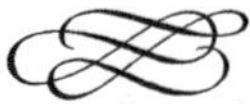

The journey to Castle Dark Forest takes about two days. We travel by train, me and the escort that King Gene has sent to make sure that I arrive at the castle safely. Some of the packs are in a bit of an uproar over the way that King Gene has chosen the four Alphas to be considered to replace him, and there's a possibility that they might be willing to take their outrage out on the women coming to the castle.

This entire journey all a little overwhelming, and I still haven't gotten my mind wrapped around why I'm even going to the castle. The last thing on earth I want to do is be a Breeder–not even for one Alpha, let alone four strangers.

My hands are trembling, and my stomach is in knots as I swallow back bile. I can't believe I'm even here!

My shoulder still hurts from where my father pushed me onto the train, right before the door closed.

This is the last place in the world I ever wanted to be!

But here I am, sitting next to Delta Sebastian, my escort, on a train speeding toward the castle. I know that there are other women on board who are going for the same purpose, but I haven't met any of them yet. The escorts all think it would be best if we wait until we get to the castle to get to know one another.

If we even have the chance to. After all, only one of us will be staying. We're all essentially competitors.

I overhear a conversation between two passengers in front of us. "I suppose some of these pretty girls must be going to the castle to audition for that dreadful Breeder position," the woman says.

The man sitting next to her, who I assume is her husband, says, "Yes, this is the third train ride I've been on this month where there's been a bunch of hopeful young women about to have their dreams shattered."

That's true. My dreams will indeed be shattered if I am selected.

But I look around the train and see lots of girls seemingly much more confident than I am. Bleached blondes, fierce redheads, girls with satiny dark hair…. I'd go as far to say that they're more beautiful than me, and because of that, I'm hopeful that one of them will be chosen, not me.

To be fair, I am not ugly, but I'm not beautiful. At least, no one has ever told me that I am. I have blonde, straight hair, blue eyes, and a decent figure. My nose is a little too long for my face, I think, and there's a small gap between my two front teeth. When I look at these other girls, I see no flaws whatsoever.

My eyes land on a redhead in a green dress. She smiles at me, and I manage a smile back, but I'm too nervous to keep looking at her. She's way prettier than I am, which makes me feel slightly better.

Everyone else seems happy about this possibility, though a few girls look a little nervous, but no one looks like they are on the verge of throwing up, like I am.

The redhead is so beautiful, she'll definitely get the job before I will, which is reassuring, because as much as my parents seem to hate me, at least I would legitimately lose instead of just having to run away to avoid the contest.

But then… maybe that is my best option. I look around the train, wondering if there's any way I can just hurl myself out one of these windows. We are going too fast for that. That doesn't mean I won't continue to consider running away if the chance presents itself.

Whatever is out there in the world, it has to be better than this.

We arrive at the train station near the castle, and we are escorted to SUVs to make the trip to the king's home, which we can see in the distance. Our escorts are still with us, so we try to keep chatting minimal. I find myself sitting right next to the same redhead. She seems nice. There's a girl with blonde curly hair across from me, and she doesn't look so welcoming.

The castle grows larger and larger as we travel toward it. I can hardly believe how huge it is.

Made of stone, it juts out of the ground and has to be at least ten stories tall in places. With turrets and catwalks on the roof, it looks daunting as the sun reflects off of its surface.

We go through a guarded gate, and the vehicle stops out front. I wait my turn to get out and then follow the other girls inside.

We are led to a waiting room, the room lined up with chairs.

"Take a seat," a woman in a black suit with a no-nonsense face, tells us. "The king will interview each of you, and then you'll go for your examination." She turns and walks away.

My eyes widen. Examination? There's a test?

One of the blondes I saw on the train leans over to a brunette and whispers, "What kind of a test do we have to take?"

The other girl laughs. "Our medical examinations, silly." She rolls her eyes, and I am glad I didn't ask the stupid question.

Our escorts have left us, so there are just the twelve of us in the waiting area now. We can talk freely, but I'm not sure I want to. It's not as if we will all be staying here. Only one of us will get the job, and the others will leave. Not to mention, this isn't even the first group of us—apparently. So who knows if it will even be someone from this group?

"I'm so nervous," the redhead whispers to me. "I think I'm going to be sick."

I think about when I threw up at the sewage treatment plant. "Yeah, me, too."

"I mean… it'll make such a huge difference to my family if I get this," she adds.

I try not to stare at her. I don't really care about how much this will help my family–I don't want the job. I silently hope she gets it.

The girl on my other side has brown hair and wide brown eyes. "I know," she says, as if the redhead had been speaking to her. "I just want to get this part over with and find out what's going to happen!"

"Why don't they just choose four of us anyway, one breeder for each Alpha?" asks the redhead to whoever was listening. "There are plenty of women here to find four suitable Breeders."

"That wouldn't be fair!" says the brunette. "What if one were more fertile than the others? Since the first to breed will be the new Alpha King, it's only fair to just have one woman!"

They all break into a discussion until the door in front of us opens, and I realize one of us is about to be called in to meet the king.

Looking around the group, I try to guess who it will be.

"Rose Forrest?" the woman in the black suit calls.

I am first?

I am first!

All eyes are on me as I stand, straightening out the red dress I am wearing. My eyes dart to the exit. Do I have enough time to run out that door instead of going into the king's office?

Not in these damn shoes!

Swallowing back my fear, I walk to the door. I try not to trip over my silver heels. I'm not used to wearing them. My parents insisted that I wear something like this, but I'm used to sneakers and jeans.

I walk into a large office and see an older man sitting behind a huge desk. He has gray and brown hair and a tight-lipped expression on his face, no smile. I bow as I've been taught. "Your Majesty," I say.

"Sit, girl," he says to me, and I walk to one of the chairs across from him. "What is your name?"

I tell him. "Rose Forrest, sir, from Elm pack."

"And how old are you?"

I swallow hard. "Twenty, sir."

"And have you found your wolf?"

I shake my head. "Not yet, sir."

He looks disappointed. I'm not twenty-one yet. If I haven't met my wolf by then, I will be worried.

"Why are you here, dear?"

My parents prepared an answer for me, but it isn't the truth, so it will be all jumbled if I try to recite it. So I tell the truth. "My parents wanted me to come, sir."

"Your parents? You don't want to be here?"

"Uh… it is an honor to meet you, Your Majesty, but I am here because my parents wanted me to come. They believe this will be a great honor. Which it will be!" I add. "But… they are the ones who are most excited about the potential."

I wish I could tell him how awful I am, but I don't know if my parents will get information about my answers, so I have to be careful not to sound like I'm trying too hard not to be chosen.

He stares at me for a long moment, his dark eyes seemingly unimpressed. "Have you been with a man before?"

I shake my head. "No, sir. Never." My cheeks flame up at the question. I hope he doesn't ask me any more intimate questions.

He looks down at his desk where he has a list of questions. He asks me, "Have you found your fated mate? Or do you have a man at home that you are in love with?"

"No, Your Majesty," I tell him. "I have no fated mate, nor am I in love with any man. I've never even been on a date with a man."

I realize once the words have escaped my lips that I've spoken too much. I hope he thinks there's something wrong with me. I can't tell him I don't have time to date because I'm too busy trying to earn money for my parents. I certainly won't mention the sewage treatment plant.

He looks me over, and I feel myself turning red in the face. A moment later, he says, "You may go."

"Thank you, Your Majesty," I say, standing. I bow and back out of the room as I've been taught.

When I'm in the hallway, the woman in the black suit says, "Head straight down that hallway to the nurse."

"Yes, ma'am," I say. I hazard one last look over at the other girls. The redhead smiles at me, but I can barely get my mouth to cooperate enough to smile back at her.

I head down the hallway to the nurse, dreading the examination that will be next. If the king doesn't like me, why even bother with this?

My mind is swimming as I think about what will happen to me next. The last thing I want is some stranger's hands all over my body.

Tears cloud my eyes as I continue to walk. I wipe them away, but more just replace them.

Why can't I just go home?

With tears clouding my vision, and terror beginning to well up inside of me, I'm not paying attention to where I'm going, and after a bit, I start to wonder if maybe I passed the examination room.

I turn around and look back, but I don't see anything. When I turn around again, I begin quickening my pace, until suddenly, I collide into a solid wall.

Made of muscle.

CHAPTER 3: RESCUED BY PURE MUSCLE

Whatever I've run into, it's solid as a rock and jars me backward, almost making me fall flat onto the stone floor of the castle.

But at the last moment, as I am tumbling backward, a hand stretches out and grabs my arm, keeping me from toppling over and pulling me back to my feet.

With tears still in my eyes, it's hard for me to see what's happening. I wipe them away with my free hand and look up into a pair of blue eyes so intense, I think I might have wandered into another realm. I've never seen a shifter with eyes like his before.

"Are you all right?" he says, but he's not the one who is holding on to me. Next to him is another man with rich chocolate-brown eyes and a concerned look on his handsome face. His fingers are wrapped around my upper arm, and his other hand is extended, in case he should need to help me find my footing again, I assume.

I'm fine now, though. Just shocked. "Y-yes," I manage to eke out, looking from one of them to the other. Never have I ever seen even one man this handsome before, and now I'm staring at two of them.

The one with the blue eyes is a bit taller than the other, with sandy blond hair and an intense stare. They are both muscle-bound, but I would say he's a little leaner than the other one. My brown-eyed rescuer has dark hair, a closely trimmed beard, and mustache. He is a little shorter than the other man, but his shoulders are wider.

Both of them are made of pure muscle and dressed like royalty in nice suit pants and white-button down shirts. The blond has on a matching black jacket. Their suits probably cost more than my house.

"Sorry," the one I've run into, the one with blue eyes, says.

"It's okay," I say back to him. He's clearly a man of few words. He seems nice, though. I am surprised at how nice people are here—for the most part. Not everyone, though.

They are nicer than my parents... so far.

"Do you need help with something?" the other one asks. He gives me a polite smile, and for a moment, I think he might be checking me out. His eyes drop down to my chest and then lower, making it to the floor before they slowly filter back up.

"Uh... I'm looking for the... medical examination room," I stammer as he finally releases my arm. My bicep suddenly feels cold without his warm fingers there, and I can feel little pulses of electricity leftover from his touch.

"Down there," blue eyes says, pointing over his shoulder. So I haven't gone far enough.

"Thank you," I manage to say. I want to speak more, but I can't get any more words out.

"You look upset," the dark-haired one notices. "Is something troubling you, miss?"

He's so polite, it takes me by surprise. Even though my father is an Alpha, I'm not used to being treated like I matter. "Oh, uh, I'm fine," I admit. "Just... nervous, I guess."

"You here for the position?" the blond asks.

He doesn't have to specify which position. We all know what he's referring to. I nod my head.

"Cool," the other one says. My eyes go to his face, and he is grinning at me. It is a lopsided grin that might look creepy on some guys, but when it is someone so attractive wearing that expression, it is endearing.

I want to ask him what he means by that. Why is it cool? Why does he care why I am here? He looks like he must be someone important, but I don't dare try to guess who. He could be a Beta or one of the king's advisors for all I know.

"I apologize for running into you, sir," I say to the man who has likely left an imprint of his pec on my forehead.

He snickers. "No problem. It's Mark."

"Mark?" I repeat, like my mouth has never formed those sounds in one string before.

"That's right." He is still smiling at me, but it seems like something I've said or done has amused him.

"And I'm Tristan," the other one says.

"Hi." That's all I'm capable of speaking. I feel lightheaded, either by their handsomeness or because I'd hit my head moments before. I can't tell. Maybe both.

They exchange amused expressions before Tristan asks me, "What is your name, sweetie?"

Sweetie? I don't think anyone has ever called me that before. It sounds nice when he says it, though. "Uh…." My name won't come out of my mouth. It's as if I don't have one.

"You do have a name don't you?" Tristan asks me, and they both chuckle again.

"Yes," I finally get out. "It's Rose. I'm Rose." I can feel my face turning the same shade as my dress. How can I not remember my own stupid name? My father's right. I am an idiot.

"That's a beautiful name," Tristan says. "Like a flower."

I arch an eyebrow. I've never heard of a Rose flower, but I'll take the compliment. "Thank you, sir."

His smile widens. "And you're so polite, too. Well, Rose, we won't keep you. I'm sure you're in a rush to get this examination over. But it sure was nice to meet you."

I nod. "You as well." I look from one of them to the other. Mark nods at me, too, like he agrees.

Still feeling flushed, I step around them and continue on my way, but I only make it a few steps down the hallway before I'm compelled to turn and look back over my shoulder at them.

They haven't moved, and they are both staring at me. Tristan waves. I don't lift my hand, though. I'm so embarrassed at being caught peeking! I turn around again and rush off, hoping my face isn't as red as it feels. My cheeks are scorching.

As I walk, I ponder who those two gentlemen might be. They were so handsome and well-bred. I have to wonder. Is it possible they might've been two of the Alphas?

"Surely not," I mutter to myself. Alphas wouldn't want to have anything to do with someone like me. The fact that they seemed to think I was attractive is astonishing to say the least. None of the boys back home ever looked at me twice. But then... I was the Alpha's daughter, and they probably feared my father.

I arrive at the examination room and pause outside, taking a deep breath.

I don't want to go in. The idea of some stranger probing my body, touching me in places I've never even touched myself... it's horrifying.

For once in my life, home seems like a better place than where I am.

I look around. Is there any place for me to run to? Maybe I could hide and then just hop back on the train when it leaves the castle.

But no... I have no choice but to move forward. My parents are expecting this of me, and even if I don't feel that I owe them anything after the way they've treated me, I've agreed to do this for my pack. I just don't understand why it is always me who has to take on these horrible situations for them.

For my pack's sake. That's at least enough to keep me motioning through the steps.

Somehow, I manage to get my feet moving forward again, and I walk through the doors, into the examination room where everything is white, sterile, and smells like bleach.

All thoughts of the two handsome gentlemen are brushed aside, and all I can think about is how badly I want to get out of here. I don't want to go home, back to my awful parents, but I do want to leave.

The thought of running away comes to my mind again. Would living on the streets be so bad compared to living with my parents? Somehow, I doubt it.

But I can't get away now… so I have to continue.

A woman dressed in a nurse's uniform comes out from behind a desk. "Ah, there you are!" she says, pursing her lips at me. "We've been waiting for nearly ten minutes."

"I-I'm sorry," I stammer. So much for everyone here being nice.

"Did you get lost, dear?" she asks, and when she says "dear" it does not sound like a term of endearment.

I nod. "Yes, sorry," I mutter.

She shakes her head at me. "It's really not that difficult. Just down the hall from the king's office."

"Yes, ma'am," I stutter.

She shakes her head at me. "Rose Forrest?"

I nod again. It's better than having to speak since my words have been failing me today.

"Very well. Go into examination room two, strip down, and put on a gown. Your doctor will be in shortly."

Again, I find my eyes fixated and my feet unable to move. I am staring at her like she's just told me to cut my own head off with a butter knife.

"Well?" she demands. "Are you stupid or hard of hearing?" she asks, reaching out and grabbing my shoulder and giving me a shove.

On my wobbly heels, I am not prepared for this, and I career forward, almost face-planting on the stone floor. Somehow, I manage to catch myself on the wall before I fall and knock my teeth out.

She grumbles, "May as well take that one off of the list." Then, raising her voice she yells, "Go!"

I figure out how to get my feet untangled and moving again, making my way down the hallway. I can't remember which room she said to go into, though, so I head for the first one and hope that's right.

Forget what I said before about doing this for my pack! It's terrible here, besides Mark and Tristan of course, but surely, they don't have a big part in all this.

I have never been happy living at home with my parents. They are always so mean to me, and they make me feel like I can't do anything right, but at this moment, more than anything in the world–I just want to leave here, even if it means I have to go back to them.

I'd even go back to the sewage treatment center if I had to.

I close the curtain and spy the gown on the table. With a deep breath, I reach around and unzip my dress.

The torment is just beginning.

CHAPTER 4: THE EXAMINATION GONE TERRIBLY WRONG

I am naked, on a bed, and my legs are spread wide open. This is how I wait for the doctor. How attractive....

The lovely nurse from before has just left. She came into the examination room to check on me, saying that she wasn't sure I could manage by myself since, clearly, I have rocks for brains, and when she arrived, she said that the doctor would be in in a moment, so I may as well go ahead and put my feet in the stirrups.

That was at least five minutes ago.

Thankfully, I have a sheet draped over my legs, and the gown I have on covers the top of me.

I stare up at a bright light, wondering if this might burn my corneas if I have to stay here much longer. That would be a great excuse to use to get sent away. Maybe then, I'll have the opportunity to run away and strike out on my own.

I am imagining the doctor will be an eighty-year-old man with cold hands and the same attitude that the nurse had. That would be my luck.

Why is it that no one who works at the castle is nice?

Tristan and Mark are nice.... Mark was quiet, but not in a rude way. And Tristan was overly friendly. I like them both, but they aren't workers here, it seems. Perhaps in another life, we could be friends–or something.

I can't help the physical reaction that happens inside of me when I think about either one of them. I start to feel myself becoming damper and damper between my spread thighs, and a tiny ache begins low beneath my belly.

Realizing I don't want the doctor to catch me in such a state, I decide to think about something else–anything else. The last thing I need is for the doctor to realize something has me excited.

I envision myself back at the sewage treatment facility and how embarrassing it was the day that I threw up.

There, that does the trick. No matter what happens, I must keep my mind off of those two guys I bumped into until this examination is over so the doctor won't see the evidence of my true feelings.

A few moments after I've steeled my resolve, I hear the curtain fly open. "Hello!" a friendly female voice says, and I look up to see a small woman, perhaps only about five feet tall, with dark hair pulled back in a bun and small spectacles balanced on the end of her nose. She is wearing a lab coat and carrying a clipboard.

"Hi," I manage to get out of my dry mouth. Talking is not my strong suit today.

"Sorry to keep you waiting, dear. I'm Dr. Penderghan. How are you, honey?" She smiles down at me, standing near my head.

I don't know how to answer that, so I finally give her the truth. "Terrified."

"Oh, dear!" she says, patting my shoulder. "I'm so sorry. I know this isn't easy. But I'll try to have you out of here as quickly as possible, all right?"

I am beginning to think I have gone into the wrong examination room because she is awfully nice, and so far, I haven't had the sort of luck that brings me nice people. Well, other than the two muscle men.

"Okay," I say, hoping she's telling the truth so I can leave.

"Now, I just need to check a few things, dear, make sure you're in good shape if the king decides to make you our lucky winner." She smiles at me like I am here for some sort of a contest and not as a favor to my entire pack. But then… I suppose most of the other girls would think of themselves as winners if they are chosen.

Not me. That would make me the biggest loser.

"All right. First I'm going to do a physical exam, and then I'll use the ultrasound machine. I'll have Nurse Maria come in to observe so you can feel comfortable that everything is fine, all right dear?"

I nod, but if Nurse Maria was the mean lady I'd met before, I don't want her in here.

Dr. Penderghan sticks her head out of the curtain and calls for Nurse Maria. A moment later, another older woman walks in. It isn't the same nurse as before, thank the Moon Goddess.

"All right," the doctor says, and I focus my eyes on the ceiling trying to put myself somewhere else as she goes about her physical examination.

It's not as bad as I think it's going to be. She basically just checks to see whether or not I am a virgin. Satisfied that I am, she moves on.

"Now, this ultrasound machine will just give us a good look at your reproductive organs," she says. "Sorry the gel is cold."

My gown is pulled up, but the sheet is still over my bottom portion, and she's told me I can take my feet out of the stirrups, thank goodness.

She's right–the gel is cold. She rubs it all over my stomach with a wand, and then the machine comes to life, and her eyes are glued on that as she moves the wand around.

After a few moments, Dr. Penderghan makes a sound like she's trying to suck all of the oxygen out of the room.

Alarmed, I turn my eyes to the screen. I hadn't been watching before because I have no idea what I should be looking at. I still don't.

"Nurse Maria, do you see what I see?" Dr. Penderghan says, her voice a sharp whisper.

Nurse Maria comes over next to me and stares at the little screen. She inhales loudly too.

"That's… amazing!" she says.

"I know!" Dr. Penderghan agrees. "One in a million!"

I swallow hard. I have no idea what they're talking about, but it sounds like they are happy about it. All I can think about is that whatever is on that screen is probably not helping me earn my ticket out of this awful place.

Dr. Penderghan puts the wand down, clicks off the machine, pulls out a few photographs she's apparently printed, and turns to me as Nurse Maria wipes the gel off of my skin. "Have you ever had an exam like this before, dear?"

I shake my head. No words are coming out of my mouth.

"Well, you have a very unusual anatomical trait that most women do not have. You have two uterine horns, dear. Like a wolf. Most shifters only have one uterus, like a human."

"Ookay," I mutter. "So… what does that mean?"

"It means your chances of conceiving are very, very good," she says with a wide smile.

I can only stare at her.

Selfishly, this is terrible news for me.

There's a bustle around me as they discuss what to do. I am in a trance, wondering exactly what this means for me.

"Get dressed, dear," Dr. Penderghan tells me, and then they both leave. And I am alone.

With my two uterine horns….

I pull myself up off of the table and get dressed, sitting back down to hook my shoes. A few moments later, Dr. Penderghan calls, "Are you dressed, dear?"

"Yes," I tell her, and she pulls the curtain open.

"The king would like to see you immediately, honey. I will walk with you."

My head rocks back and forth, and I press my feet to start moving like I'm some sort of automaton or zombie.

Dr. Penderghan is overjoyed as she walks down the hallway with me. She is practically humming with excitement. I don't know what to think about any of this. Perhaps King Gene will think I am some sort of an abomination from how I'm walking and send me straight home.

We do not enter the king's office as I expected. Instead, we head towards a large auditorium, and Dr. Penderghan walks me up on stage.

Bright lights shine into my eyes, but as I look out at the crowd, I can tell that there are dozens, maybe hundreds of people out there. I can't see many faces, but I can see the front row. I recognize the red-headed girl I spoke to before and that blonde who was so stuck up.

Why are all of these people here?

Why am I here?

"This is her?" King Gene says to the doctor as we walk over to him. He looks shocked to see me again so soon.

"Yes, Your Majesty," she says and hands him the pictures.

He looks at them and makes the same annoying 'ahh' sound like the doctor and nurse had done. "Very well," he says. "Thank you, Doctor."

Dr. Penderghan nods her head, and then steps back beside me as King Gene quiets the crowd.

"Ladies, gentlemen, and all citizens of the kingdom," he begins as the crowd quiets to a hum, and I find myself looking out at the audience as well. "It is with great pleasure that I announce to you that our Breeder has been found!"

I look around. Is there another woman on the stage? Who is she?

Then... he answers the question for me. "Rose Forrest of Elm pack!" He is gesturing at me!

I'm the Breeder? Because of my stupid abnormal uterus? That's all it takes? Really?!

I don't even know how to react. My knees are threatening to give way. All I want to do is to run down off of the stage and hide some-where—anywhere.

But I'm here, and I can't. There are guards for one thing. Also, my parents would murder me if I came home now. News travels fast here and when they found out I had been selected and had managed to outrun the king's guard, they wouldn't accept me back in their house. They would beat me out in the streets like a stray dog caught stealing food.

I try to refocus my attention on the room around me. Many people in the crowd are clapping and cheering, but on some of the other girls' faces, I see outrage.

"What?" I hear a voice shriek, and I look out to see it is the blonde from before. "No fucking way!" she screams.

"Calm down, Kerry," a brunette next to her says, looking around to see if the guards are moving in on Kerry. The brunette has to rub Kerry's back to stop the girl's hyperventilating.

I know who she is now. Kerry Hill. From Brush pack. Her father, Alpha Robert, is one of the most powerful Alphas in the kingdom.

It's no wonder she's mad. She probably feels she deserves to be the one to carry the future heir and maybe even marry the next king.

They won't expect me to do that, will they?

I can't even think about what all of this means!

Kerry is escorted from the auditorium, along with a few other angry girls who are interrupting the king. I wonder if they will be punished for getting out of line, but I doubt it. They should be given some leniency for coming all this way and not getting what they'd hoped for. Like some sort of participation award that says, 'Breeder Tournament: Runner-Up.'

Now that's something tangible I can brag about. Not two uterine horns....

"Thank you all for coming," King Gene continues. "Now... you may all go!"

For a moment, I hope that I am somehow included in that statement.

But it doesn't last. He turns to me and says, "Except for you, of course." A wicked smile pulls

back his parted lips, and panic washes over me.

What have I gotten myself into?

CHAPTER 5: THE LUNA SUITE

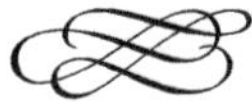

King Gene dismisses everyone from the auditorium except for me.

Dr. Penderghan stays with me, and I notice a couple standing down at the bottom of the stage. Still, my heart is pounding in my chest. I wonder what in the world is going to happen to me now.

"Well, I must say," the Alpha King begins as soon as we are mostly alone, "when I met you earlier, I was not expecting you to be the winner."

I can only stare at him. Believe me, I wasn't either!

"But once Dr. Penderghan told me of your unique situation, well, how could I choose anyone else?" He smiles at me again, and like before, I feel my stomach tighten. I don't like that smile.

It's... creepy and makes me question his sincerity.

"I think that she's a bit overwhelmed," Dr. Penderghan says, resting her hand on my shoulder.

"Perhaps we should let her have a rest before you introduce her to the Alphas?"

King Gene is still staring at me, and I've felt his eyes wandering along my form as the doctor is speaking. When that handsome man in the hallway did that earlier, it made me feel attractive and beautiful. But this makes me feel almost as creepy as his smile.

"Yes, yes, of course," the king finally says. "Beta Adam! Can you and Shelby escort Miss Rose to her room?"

"Yes, Alpha," the man who is still standing at the edge of the stage answers. I look at him closely for the first time and see he isn't much older than me. I had no idea that the Beta was so young.

Perhaps he hasn't been the Beta for long? No one ever speaks of the Alpha King's Beta.

He gestures for me to meet him at the stairwell, and I realize, with the king in the room, I'll have to back down the stairs.

In these shoes, that seems dangerous.

I'm not supposed to turn my back on the king, though.

Thankfully, before I make it to the edge of the stairs, the king turns and walks off in the other

direction.

Thank the Moon Goddess!

Beta Adam offers me his hand, and I take it. He helps guide me down the stairs as I hold up my gown with the other hand.

"Hello, Miss Rose," he says to me in a kind voice. He is quite good-looking himself, though not as handsome as the men I met in the hall-way. He's tall and strong with reddish-blond hair and kind green eyes. My body doesn't feel a spark when I'm around him, but I'm happy to at least have another friendly face to add to my circle seeing as I might be stuck here for a while.

"Hello," I say to him, realizing I'm shaking a bit. I'm so nervous about all of this. I can hardly even wrap my mind around what's happening.

Am I really going to be the Breeder for four men??

"This is my wife, Shelby," he says and the woman who was standing near him earlier walks over. She's adorable, with a button nose and apple cheeks. Her hair is a bit more brunette than his but still with shades of red. She has a smattering of freckles across her nose. I think she is probably just a few years older than me.

"Hello," I greet her. "It's nice to meet you."

"You, too," she says with a smile, and instead of shaking my hand, she loosely wraps her arms around me, like we are already long-time friends. "I'm so excited to get to know you!"

Dr. Penderghan pats my back and says, "I shall see you soon, dear," before she heads off to the

exit.

I hear Adam mutter to Shelby, "Calm down, honey. Don't overwhelm her."

"I'm sorry," Shelby apologizes. "It's just… there aren't a lot of women here around our age. Except for the maids, and the king prefers that we don't fraternize with them if we can help it."

"I understand," I sympathize, forcing a smile. It isn't that I don't appreciate the fact that she wants to be my friend. I don't have a lot of friends, none that I'm even going to miss, so it would be great to have a friend here. But I am so nervous, I can't even think, let alone try to be happy.

"Shall we?" Beta Adam says, and I nod, following him.

Shelby walks beside me, and as we go, she asks me questions about my family and my life back home. I can only give her short answers. Words seem to stick in my throat. It might be a condition I need to ask Dr. Penderghan about later, but I self-diagnose it as my mind still trying to compute that this is my home now—for the moment anyway.

We walk down long winding hallways that seem to all look the same, and I wonder how in the world I'll ever figure out how to make my way around here on a daily basis.

"Don't worry, you'll figure out the hallways," Shelby assures, as if reading my mind.

"I hope so," I say, but I'm not sure, and a bit frightened that she knew my thoughts so easily.

We turn down another hallway, and Beta Adam pulls up.

There's a man there, coming toward us from down the narrow hall, walking rather quickly. He has dark hair and a muscular build—that seems to be a theme around here—much like the other two men I ran into earlier. His chiseled jaw is set, and he looks annoyed. His dark eyes are glued to the floor, and he only looks up in time to step around us.

"Beg your pardon, Adam," he says.

"No problem, sir," the Beta replies, and then I find the attractive man staring at me.

He scans me up and down for a second as we stop in the hallway, the four of us just standing there.

Finally, he greets, "Hi," and I manage to feign a smile at him, but I don't know what to say.

"Congratulations. You must be excited."

"Uh… yeah," I choke out. I guess he knows who I am then. I have no idea who he is, but judging by his suit and his overall appearance, I'm guessing he is important.

"Thousands of girls wanted the job you just won," he continues, his tone becoming friendly the more he talks. Maybe he wasn't in such a hurry after all.

I am not sure what to say to that, so I just stand there… like an idiot.

He chuckles at me. "Well, I hope that you can get over your nervousness soon. You have no reason to be scared." He pats me on the arm, and the touch of his hand sends electrical impulses all up and down my skin.

"Th-thanks," I stutter.

"See you later."

I'm not sure if he's talking to me or Adam or all three of us, so I say nothing, but when he withdraws his hand to carry along on his way, my arm feels cold, like it's meant to have his hand on it.

Shelby giggles. "Isn't he dreamy?"

Before I can respond, Beta Adam clears his throat. "You know I can hear you, right?"

"Oh, Adam!" she says rushing up to grab his hand. "You know I think you're the dreamiest of all!"

Poor Beta Adam. He looks over to me for backup but I don't want to lie. I remain silent.

By the time Shelby returns her attention to me, I feel it's too late for me to speak. So I say nothing.

But yes... I do think that man was dreamy.

Whoever he was.

A few minutes later, we arrive at a large wooden double door, carved with flowers and filled with gold inlay.

It's beautiful.

"Here we are," Beta Adam announces, pushing the door open.

I stand outside and stare for a moment, first at the door... and then at the room.

It's gorgeous–and huge. I think most of my house back home would fit in here.

There's a living room area with a large plush red sofa set before an expansive television set.

The sitting area is nice and inviting, despite the bold colors. The rug on the rich wooden floor is also red with gold accents. My eyes follow it over to the bedroom area where a huge four-poster bed with a red canopy and matching silky red bedspread invites me to collapse and take a nap.

All of the woods are a rich brown color with red tints.

Behind Beta Adam, there are three huge floor-to-ceiling windows with matching red and gold drapes. I can't see outside just yet because of the angle, other than the bright azure sky. I can't wait to rush over and see if there's a garden view. That would be lovely.

"This is great, isn't it?" Shelby asks. "The king had it done up as a second Luna suite. Oh, and in there is your bathroom! All white marble with a jetted tub big enough for at least two! Who will be the lucky man?" Shelby giggles coquettishly.

My eyebrows arch. I would love to sit in it...alone if possible.

I notice that the room matches my dress and wonder if that's just a coincidence. It would have to be, I suppose.

"It's beautiful," I tell them.

She walks over to an armoire and pulls it open. "There's a ton of clothes in here. I think you will find that everything is in your size, but if not, let us know, and we'll get you the right fit."

All I can say is, "Thank you." It probably makes me seem unappreciative given the room that was just offered to me, but, you know, I didn't ask for any of this.

She smiles at me and closes the armoire door.

"Well... I'm sure you're probably tired," Beta Adam says. "We'll get your luggage from your escort and make sure that you have your things from home."

I haven't brought much, but I would like to have the little I did pack. "Thank you." That seems to be all I can say.

"Of course. You'll have some servants, but we'll give you a chance to rest before we bring them in to meet you. If you do require anything, just pick up the phone and dial nine." He gestures to the gold antique-style telephone on the nightstand.

"Thank you...."

He smiles at me and then gestures for Shelby. "Come on, honey."

She walks back over to me first. Wrapping me up in another hug, she squeezes tighter this time.

"I'm so glad you're here," she says before the two of them give me a little wave and leave the room.

I am alone–and I feel it. Even though Shelby is nice, and I've met some very attractive men who seem to be interested in me, it doesn't matter because I have no idea who they are. And I still haven't met the four men I'm meant to bed.

My eyes go to that piece of furniture. All I want to do is fall asleep and wake up back at home.

I sit down on the edge and take off my shoes, but I'm too afraid to change clothes since I have no idea when I might be summoned. I lay down on top of the blanket that matches my dress and close my eyes, wondering what will happen next.

CHAPTER 6: RULES OF ENGAGEMENT

Reece

I'm almost late.

I didn't really have time after the king's announcement to duck out of the auditorium and make it all the way back to my room, but I realized I was underdressed when I saw the other three Alphas standing in suits in the back of the room. When the king asked us to meet with him, I figured I shouldn't be the only one in jeans and a polo.

So… I'd rushed back to my room to change. Now, I have to rush to get back to the king's office for our meeting.

But I'm glad I went.

It gave me a chance to see the girl up close.

She's beautiful… and even though I know she's nervous and probably a little scared, it's quite clear that she is as attracted to me as I am to her.

That will come in handy…. If King Gene said that I had to bed an unattractive woman just because she was the healthiest of the pack or the most well-bred, I would protest.

But this girl was gorgeous, and I didn't even care whose daughter she was at this point. I just wanted to see her again. When my hand rested on her arm, I felt a warmth radiate up to my elbow. It was like I was meant to touch her.

I rush into the room with less than a minute to spare and find I'm the last one to arrive.

"Hey, Reece!" Tristan says, a crooked grin on his face. "Nice of you to join us." I growl at him and take my seat at the end, on the other side of Mark. The others look amused, except for the king. He doesn't seem annoyed that I'm almost late, but he isn't happy either.

But then… King Gene is never happy.

"Sorry, Sir," I mutter.

"You're fine," he says. "I just wanted to go over the rules with the four of you, to make sure you're clear on my expectations and what I plan to do in terms of determining who will be my heir. All four of you have proven yourselves to be loyal to me. You're good leaders, brave warriors, and attractive men. A child any of you produces with this girl will be an asset to the

kingdom. So… that's it. That's how we will decide the heir."

"Whoever impregnates her first?" Eli asks, running his hand through his red hair.

"That's right," the king says. "In order to determine the order in which you will have your first try, we will have a race, in your wolf forms, tomorrow afternoon. Whoever comes in first will have first dibs on her and claim her virginity."

I feel a flicker in my groin at the mention of the girl's virginity. She's never been claimed at all?

Intriguing.

I don't like the idea of sharing her with these other three men, but at least we won't have to share her with anyone else.

"I hope that all of you will promise not to sleep with her out of turn. It wouldn't be fair."

The four of us nod. "Of course," I say, and the others echo. Though… I have to admit, it might be difficult to keep my hands off of her. I think of her soft curves, the roundness of her full breasts… yeah, it'll be hard, all right. I feel another tightening in my pants and have to resist the urge to readjust. Mark shifts in his seat, and I wonder if he is thinking the same thing.

"As soon as we know the girl is pregnant, we will do a test on the child to determine who the father is as soon as possible, and that man will become the next king. Then, I will retire and leave the kingdom to him."

The four of us exchange glances. We have known each other our entire lives, in one way or another, and we've become friends. I know that, whoever wins, they will be fair to the other three and reward them somehow for their loyalty. I know I will if I am the winner. These other three Alphas are the best of the best, and I respect them.

"And what of the girl?" Tristan asks. "Will the winner marry her and make her the Luna?"

King Gene laughs loudly, and I am tempted to exchange a shocked glance with the others, but none of us dare look at one another.

"Heavens, no!" he exclaims. "This girl is not fit to be a Luna! Her father is an Alpha, that's true, but Alpha Howard of Elm pack is an Alpha in name only. He's certainly not a proven leader. The girl was chosen simply because she has two uterine horns."

My forehead furrows. "Two... uterine horns?" I know what he means, but I don't understand why

that makes her the winner.

She's beautiful and seems very sweet. Why wouldn't that be enough? I assumed it was that and that she must also be quite intelligent and possibly bred from a highly ranked family.

I guess I was wrong on some of those counts....

"Yes, it will be easier for her to get pregnant," he admits. "And she's not hard to look at...." The king's expression in reaction to the girl is a bit...disconcerting. He continues, "But no, she will not be the next Luna."

We all sit in silence for a moment, almost daring one another to ask the next obvious question.

It is Mark, with his piercing blue eyes that all of the girls love so much, who speaks up, finally.

"Then… who will be?" he asks.

"Yes, who will be the Luna?" Eli also wonders.

"I have chosen a beautiful daughter of a proper Alpha to become the next Luna. You will be satisfied with her, I assure you."

He seems to be done speaking, and we still don't know who he is talking about.

Tristan speaks up. "May we know her name?"

He nods. "Emily Ivy."

I bite back the gasp that threatens to slip from my lips.

Emily Ivy. Daughter of Alpha Lawrence Ivy of Brook pack.

The king's cousin's daughter….

"Was Emily considered as the Breeder?" Eli asks.

The king's eyes widen as if he's asked an obscene question. "Goddess, no!" he says. "Do you think I'd defile my family by allowing my cousin's daughter to sleep with four different men? No, my cousin's daughter is as pure as the freshly fallen snow on the top of a mountain's peak, and she shall remain that way until she is married to whoever wins this contest."

That answers that question….

"Yes, Sir. I'm sorry," Eli apologizes, bowing his head.

"No need," King Gene waves him off, but it's clear he doesn't mean it. He's annoyed. "Now, I ask that the four of you stay away from her the best you can until after the run. Then, we shall see what order you will have her in. Please, manage your turns as is decided upon. This needs to be as fair as possible."

"Yes, Alpha King," we all say in unison.

King Gene dismisses us with a wave of his hand, and the four of us stand to walk out of his office. I want to tell the other three that I saw her in the hallway, but I don't want to make them jealous.

"Can you believe it?" Tristan says, brushing a hand through his brown hair. "It's the same girl we talked to in the hallway!"

"I know. It's crazy," Mark agrees.

"Wait–the two of you spoke to her already?" Eli asks, his face turning almost as red as his hair. "Well, that's not fair."

"I did, too," I admit.

All three turn to look at me as we slowly make our way back to our rooms, which are quite a ways away from the office.

"You did?" Eli asks me. "When?"

"On my way back from changing my clothes. I hardly said anything to her, and she was too nervous to really speak. I'm not sure she knew who I was."

"I don't think she knew who we were either," Mark says.

"Well, that's just great!" Eli says. "I'm already at a disadvantage, and we haven't even started yet!"

"Relax, Eli," Tristan says. "It's not like we impregnated her by saying hello."

"I tried," I say, and they all snicker at my joke. "I guess my eyes just aren't as piercing as Mark's."

That gets another laugh out of everyone, and Mark punches me in the arm. He's playing, but it still hurts. I try not to react.

"Well, you guys keep all of your piercing parts out of her until I at least get a chance to speak to her," Eli insists.

'Piercing parts.' Sounds suggestive….

We all laugh at Eli's empty threat and continue to talk about how beautiful she is until we reach our rooms.

Eli's door opens first, and a beautiful brunette, with highlights of red in her hair, steps out.

"What's so funny, brother?" she asks.

Kelly is his sister, but since we've been at the castle these past few months, she seems like she's my sister, too. All of us feel the same way.

"Nothing. Just stupid boy talk." Eli shrugs.

"Are you taking me to the gardens soon?" Kelly asks, leaning against the door jamb.

Eli sighs. "Soon," he promises her. "I need to check in with my Beta. I'm still running a pack, even though I'm not there, you know."

He has a point. I need to check with my Beta, too. I don't like leaving the pack for this long, but it's for a worthy cause, and I trust the people I've left behind. "See you all later," I say and walk the few doors down to my own room.

We are all going to do work, from the sound of it.

I need to get everything I can done before I have my first encounter with Rose.

Because I have a feeling that once I've had her, she'll be all I can think about.

CHAPTER 7: A FRIEND IN NEED

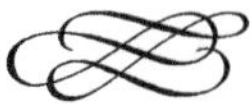

Peeking through the windows, my surprise and confusion turn to horror. Four figures stand in the dark fog in the gardens below. I blink and try to adjust my sight.

Their forms seem to be swaying to music only the four of them can hear. As my eyes focus intently on the faces looking up at me, my heart drops. I open my mouth to scream, but no sound comes out.

I have never seen a ghost, but they say there is a first time for everything. The faces below are blurry. They all have no definitive features. They are faceless.

I attempt to scream again, but like before, it seems like someone has pressed the mute button on me. I try to move away from the window. I don't want to see the scary faceless figures that are looking up at me anymore.

I find that I can't move; it's like my feet are stuck in something. I look down. Two horns have my feet pinned to the floor. My skin feels flushed, and I can feel sweat beads forming. What's happening? Where am I?

A movement behind me makes my heart leap to my throat. I struggle to find my motor skills again. I lift my gaze to the gloomy skyline outside the window, purposefully not daring to look down at the scary figures below. I glimpse the moon behind some dark clouds. I find myself asking the Moon Goddess for strength.

Suddenly, a blinding light filters over my face.

My body jerks up and I can feel a soft surface beneath me. I blink against the light. I realize I am now sitting in a bed. The room looks large and unfamiliar, but I exhale in relief because suddenly I can move. A shadow catches my peripheral vision. I yelp.

"Are you okay, my lady?" a voice asks.

I look toward the source and see a young girl almost my age looking down at me with worry in her eyes. It takes a few seconds to register fully where I am. I bring my hand up to clutch at my throat. I must have been having a nightmare.

The puzzle pieces of the full story about where I am, like magic, fall into place. I am in the castle, crowned with the displeasure of helping my family out financially by using the two uterine horn superpower genes to produce an heir for one of four Alphas.

The girl proceeds to blink at me. I can tell she is unsure about how to proceed.

"Argh, I..." I manage to stutter groggily while attempting to rub the sleep out of my eyes with the back of my hand.

The girl smiles at me. "I hope I didn't startle you. I was just drawing the blinds open."

I glare at her. My brain is trying to reboot from my uneasy slumber. What am I supposed to say? What time is it? Who is she? The light outside tells me that it is daytime. Have I slept through the night? Is it morning or afternoon? I decide not to offer any greetings because I am unsure if 'good morning' or 'good afternoon' would suffice.

"Thank you," I manage instead.

I feel like an idiot. What exactly was I thanking her for? For almost giving me a heart attack? I wipe my face again. Well, she did just save me from the most bizarre nightmare.

"I put a tray of bath salts and soaps for you in the bathroom for your bath."

"Thank you, ..." I feel like a broken record. What's her name?

As if reading my confusion telepathically, she offered, "I'm Venice. I will be your chambermaid for the duration of your stay here."

I nod. She does a small bow and walks out of the room. Alone now, I exhale and inhale. Memories of my nightmare cause me to pull the wool duvet away from my feet. I breathe with relief to find no horns growing out of them.

I swing my feet off the bed and welcome the feel of the cold ceramic tiles against my heels. I yawn and stretch my hands over my head. I can hear a few bones cracking with delight at being straightened. Slowly I tread to the bathroom while taking in more details of the room as I walk.

I gasp as I look into the bathroom. The room is almost half the size of the bedroom. The white oval jetted tub looks like a mini swimming pool, adorned with gold-encrusted plumbing. Magical!

I manage to figure out how the sophisticated buttons work and soon I have myself a warm bath.

I choose a little satin drawstring pouch marked with the words 'lavender' because I know how relaxing it can be. A sprinkle of some Epsom salts into the bath water puts the final touches to it.

I easily slip out of the red dress I hadn't bothered taking off before and step into the water.

Closing my eyes, I lean back onto the cushiony bath pillow. The lavender scent tickles my nostrils as it works its magic. I feel my muscles begin to relax and I inhale the aroma that now fills the whole room.

Suddenly, I hear footsteps coming from the bedroom. I can't help but panic. The bathroom door is ajar and here I sit, naked in the tub. I don't know how much my poor heart and mind can take. My eyes look nervously around the room trying to find something, anything to use to cover myself.

"Hi," a cheerful voice announces as a head pops through the open door. "I hope you are rested."

"I..I.." I stutter.

Shelby beams at me from the door. She doesn't seem to be bothered by the fact that I am naked. I wince as she proceeds to walk across the bathroom marble tiles toward me, using my hands to cover my exposed breasts. She perches on the rim of the tub and smiles at me. This is just awkward....

"Mmm, it smells so good in here. I hope you don't mind. Adam was summoned by the king and I had nothing to do. So when the maid told me that you were up, I decided to come over and chat. Venice–that's your head chambermaid's name."

I can feel my face heat up with embarrassment. Although we are both women, and other strangers have already eyed my most intimate nakedness, this still feels weird. Shelby doesn't seem to notice how uncomfortable I am as she reaches inside the tub and plays with the water.

"Oh," I say awkwardly.

"Your skin is gorgeous. Glistening like you were dipped in honey," she confesses.

I'm at a loss for words. I'm just not used to receiving compliments and I'm bad at reacting to them. Having never had many truly close friends, I'm not sure how friends are supposed to interact. Maybe they always hang out in bathrooms together?

I try to relax since I don't want to make Shelby feel bad. I could use an ally and confidant around here. Being alone with my own thoughts in this situation might be bad for my mental health.

"Please pass me the towel," I say and manage to smile at her. Well, so much for the long soak I had been going for.

Shelby stands up and moves to a shelf in the corner of the room and retrieves a long blue towel. When she walks back over to me, she doesn't hand it to me. Instead, she stands, holding it for me to step into. Was she planning to wrap the towel around me? I'm capable of doing that myself, but I decide to just let myself indulge in her kindness as long as she doesn't pull anything funny.

I stand up and step out of the tub cautiously. Again she is unfazed by my naked body, as she proceeds to help wrap the towel around me before fastening it in a loose knot under my raised arms.

"Thank you," I say, happy her intentions were honest.

"Uh-huh." Shelby turns around and walks out of the bathroom

into the bedroom. I follow her, feeling a bit relieved to be finally covered.

I walk over to the huge oak dressing table in the room and start moisturizing my body with the intoxicatingly great smelling shimmering citrus lotion from the huge squirt bottle sitting there.

"How have you not yet met your mate? You are gorgeous, and one would think you would have met your fated mate already."

I look at Shelby through the reflection of the dressing table mirror. She's sitting at the edge of the bed watching me.

I shrug. I have no idea how I still hadn't met my mate and how I was still a virgin. Maybe if I had, I wouldn't find myself here about to give my virginity to four Alphas who I had no deep feelings for.

My mind starts playing different scenarios. What would my first time be like with a man whose only intention was to plant his seed in me? Would he be gentle? Would there be any passion, or would he treat me exactly like what I had been reduced into–a living and breathing incubator.

CHAPTER 8: PIECES OF THE FOUR ALPHAS

Rose

We walk down the hallways with Shelby right by my side. She points at a wall to our right.

"Those are the past rulers who once lived here and ruled in these walls. Some ruled for decades. That is King David, he ruled for almost fifty years. He was a very young lad when he became king. That picture was taken during his heyday. Wasn't he a sight for sore eyes?"

I keep looking at the wall of fame, wondering which of the dozen pictures she was pointing at belongs to the king who was apparently a sight for sore eyes.

We don't stop long enough for me to ask any more questions. This castle seems to be rich with history. The décor and armory that stands as decoration along the hallways tell stories without the need for words.

If this is the same path we had taken to my room, then it seemed like it had increased in length since, because I don't remember it having been this long. I am already tired and wonder how much we still have to walk.

I'm hoping I won't have to stand through a full tour of this monstrous residence in just one day.

As we pass a French door that leads out to a balcony, I catch a glimpse of one of the men I had met earlier. He is flipping through some pages of a book and his head is preoccupied looking down at it.

Shelby stops and grabs my wrist. "That there is Tristan Stone. He is the Alpha of Hill pack. He always has his nose in one book or the other. People sometimes nickname him Einstein. Despite his intelligence, don't mistake him for a weak nerd. He is a very powerful leader and one of the Alphas that you will breed with."

I keep staring at the well-built man through the glass doors. I seem unable to tear my eyes away from the brooding biceps that are quite visible through his starched shirt.

"Is he a sociable person?" I ask before I can stop myself. Was it a good idea to be looking for personal details about their characteristics? Well, if I was going to be sharing a bed with these men, I was definitely on a need to know basis now.

It didn't matter how afraid of this situation I was. I was here–it was happening. I needed to find a way to be practical about it, at the very least.

"Well, he is somewhat quiet. Only choosing to speak when it's really necessary," Shelby replies as she takes my hand and we continue with our tour.

"Can you…uhh tell me more about all the Alphas that I am here for?"

Shelby looks at me and gives me a mischievous look. "Umm, you seem to be quite the curious one. I think I would be curious too about anyone I have to get intimate with. You will soon meet all of them though." I see a weird look flash across her face. It looks like pity.

I clear my throat. She probably pities the girl who is going to have sex with four men in succession. Well, I don't need her pity. I pity myself in bucket loads enough already as it is.

"Tell me, Rose, why are you doing this?"

Her question catches me off guard. Why does everyone else do this kind of thing? It rarely is just because they have a double horned uterus.

I wonder if I should be fully honest with her. We hardly know each other, but I figure honesty could lead to a solid friendship with her. After all, she has been nothing but nice towards me…a bit weird…but nice.

"My parents could use the money that comes from me actually doing this," I answer simply. Shelby gives me a side-way glance. I pray she doesn't give me that look laced with pity again. Somehow that look pushes me to the brink of a breakdown making me reflect on what I was actually tasked to do here.

"Is your own father not an Alpha?" Shelby asks. I chuckle a bit louder than I meant to. It seems she had done a background check on me. Not a very thorough one though, or she would have known that my father's title was just glorified without the financial success to back it up.

"Yes, he is technically an Alpha, but that's the end of it. The financial success never seemed to be able to catch up to his title." And now… he'd sold me. I would never be able to forgive him for that.

Never.

Shelby nods and I think she is going to give me that look again, but instead she smiles gently. As we walk, we enter into a room where two men are sitting, seemingly in a heated debate about whose wolf form was faster than whose.

"Rose, meet Alpha Reece Gold of Canyon Pack and Alpha Mark Gray of Rapids Pack. Gentlemen, this is Rose."

I blush when I realize I had actually run into all these Alphas earlier. I had counted three so far and wondered if I had met the fourth one as well and just hadn't realized .

They are all very handsome. I doubt sharing a bed and spending a night with any of them would be so bad actually. There could be worse punishments…. I feel my face grow warmer as my trail of thoughts has already led to a bed with these dashing alphas.

"Ah, the beautiful woman from earlier graces us with her presence," Alpha Reece greets.

I feel like a fire is just burning directly on my skin now. Had this man just referred to me as beautiful? I glare at him as I shift my weight from one foot to the other. He follows my unlady-like swaying with his eyes. He doesn't appear to have impaired vision, so why did he think I was beautiful? Was he just being polite?

I smile back at him regardless of my suspicions at his compliment. "It's nice to actually put names to the faces. It's an honor to meet you both."

"Oh, I had no idea you had already met," Shelby says as she looks at all of us in succession. Her mischievous glare is back again.

Damn could my face get any hotter? The answer is yes, yes it could.

"Don't be a stranger, sweetie. Come and perch on my lap, and tell Reece here that you think I am better looking than his spoiled ass!" Now my face was on fire.

I smile politely at Alpha Mark, but make no movement towards him.

I am relieved when Shelby cuts in, "Right now, Rose is all mine. You will get your chance to have her later on."

Although she has just saved me from having to satisfy Alpha Mark's request, I feel like these Alphas only see me as a toy–a possession–who everyone here is going to have a turn at owning. Or should I say, fucking.

I bow my head slightly at the two men, and can feel their gazes on me as we walk out of the room. This whole setup is going to be interesting to say but the least.

For some reason my mind is focused on the pragmatic details of how I can possibly sleep with four different men right after another. Like is there a sleeping schedule? Is there some sort of rule I have to follow? Do I need to sign a contract?

Shelby leads me to what looks like a patio. It is paved with pea gravel that seems to glitter under the sunlight.

A beautiful woman is laughing at something a tall, broad shouldered man is saying. I cock my head to the side to listen in, but I can't make out the conversation.

The rays of sunlight on her hair makes it look like there are little sparks of fire on her head.

Now she was the definition of beautiful, not me.

I look at the man she is with and wonder who they both are. His looks are a bit plain compared to the hunks I had already met, but something about him is magnetic. He has a...kind face.

As if reading my mind, Shelby says, "That is Eli Silver. Alpha of Beach pack."

I nod and say without thinking, "Is he one of my Alphas?" I realize how I had just called them 'my Alphas,' and rush to correct myself. "I mean, is he one of the four alphas I am here for?"

Shelby throws her head back and laughs. "Yes, dear. Don't worry, for the duration of your stay here you can go ahead and call them 'your alphas.' They will all be yours anyway."

I like Shelby. She always has a way of making me feel at ease...that is when she is not ogling me while I bathe.

The man looks in our direction. His eyes shift and focus directly on me. I can feel the pull of his stare even from this far. I can't move. He raises his hand and waves. We both wave back.

"Who is that with him?" I ask.

Shelby nudges me playfully. "Is someone jealous already? That is just his sister."

"Oh." I feel relieved when a realization hits me. I need to blink to snap myself out of the fantasy that is playing out in my mind.

Am I actually feeling possessive over these men? I was just here as their breeder; they were not really my alphas in that sense.

But, why did I want them all for myself?

CHAPTER 9: SCREAMING AND CRYING

Rose

Shelby is chattering along as we walk back inside, back down the same corridors and passageways we've already gone. I nod and try to make agreeable sounds while she is talking because I don't want to be rude, but on the inside, I'm not even listening to her—I'm thinking about the Alphas.

My Alphas.

At least, that's what I'd taken to calling them for some reason I don't quite understand. It isn't as if they actually belong to me. If anything, I belong to them. Still, I can't help but think of them a little possessively as my mind goes back over their handsome faces.

They are all so interesting and appealing in their own way. All of them are physically strong, yet not any two of them looked remotely alike.

I wonder if King Gene had given any thought to that, making sure there was no dispute over who the father was. Granted, he could simply do a DNA test, but if the baby comes out with dark black hair or red locks, it will be obvious who the father was, wouldn't it?

We round a corner, and once again, I find myself running into someone. This time, the "oof" I hear is accompanied by the tinkling of breaking glass, and a hard smack on the floor that isn't me tumbling.

I look down to see that I've run into a woman. She's beautiful, with raven black hair, big brown doe eyes, and perfectly pouty red lips. Right now, though, her lips are parted, and she's screaming at me.

"What the actual fuck, bitch?" she demands as Shelby tries to help her up. A couple of other ladies rush over to help as well.

"I am so sorry!" I say. It seems that not only has she dropped a glass of wine when she fell, but it also splashed all over her gown—which was a nice cream color.

"Miss Emily, are you all right?" Shelby is asking as the woman is hauled to her feet.

"No, I'm not all right!" she shouts. "I was on my way to meet with my cousin, the king, and now… I have wine all over my dress!"

"I don't know what to say," I tell her. "It was an accident. Can I scrub it? Try to get it out?"

"Are you serious?" she asks. "This dress is made of one hundred percent silk from the finest silkworms in all of the kingdom. No, I will not let your pitiful little hands touch it." All three of the ladies are glaring at me.

Shelby tries to step in. "Miss Emily, it was an accident. We came around the corner at the same time as you. Miss Rose didn't mean—"

But the Beta's wife is cut off. "No one asked you what you think, Shelby!" Emily snapped, her eyes slitting as she focuses in on the Beta's wife.

'Wow—she was even mean to the Beta's wife! She must think she is pretty special,' I thought to myself. But then… if she's King Gene's cousin, as she says, then perhaps she is right to think that way.

I silently wonder what she's doing here. She is so ethereally beautiful and also related to the king. I wonder if she was one of the contestants for the Breeder position, but how can I ask that?

Shelby probably knows. She seems to know everything.

I will ask her later. Right now, I'm not done being screamed at by Emily.

"And if I ever see your ugly face again, I swear to the Moon

Goddess, I will grab hold of that huge schnoz of yours and rip it right off your face!"

My eyes widen in horror, and my hands immediately go to cover my nose. I've always thought it was way too long for my face, even though others have said it's just fine. Now,

I feel as if everyone has been lying to me.

"Come on, Miss Rose," Shelby says, tugging me around the mess. "We don't have to stand here and listen to this."

A maid comes with a broom and mop to clean up the mess, and I tell her, "I'm so sorry." She only bows her head and moves on.

I hear Emily shout, "Clean this all up, bitch!" Then she says, "My beautiful dress is ruined! I'm going to make that bitch pay for this!"

"I guess they can take the money out of my pay... before they send it to my family," I say as Shelby and I hear the maid scooping the glass up with the broom while the other women hurry back the way they'd come, down a side hallway, complaining about her gown still.

I really can't blame her. I'd be upset if someone ruined my dress, too, though I would never yell at them like that. Especially not if they apologized.

"Don't mind her," Shelby says. "She's all bark and no bite. You don't have to pay for her dress. The laundresses here are excellent. They'll get the stain out. One time, I was wearing a white dress to a dinner party, and someone bumped my arm, and I spilled burgundy wine all down the front, and they got it out the next day. No problem!" Shelby smiles and pats my shoulder.

"Was your dress made from the finest silk from the finest silkworms in all of the kingdom?" I ask her.

"Well, no," Shelby admits. "But it won't matter. It'll be good as new in no time. I'm sure of it."

I want to believe her, but I still feel bad. My mind is elsewhere as she continues to tell me about all of the kings and other royals whose likenesses we are passing in the hall

on the way back to my room.

At least, that's where I assume we are going.

When we reach the hallway where my room is, Beta Adam is

walking toward us, his long legs allowing him to cover the ground so much faster than either of us.

"Oh, hi, honey!" Shelby gushes, rushing to meet him. She wraps her arms around him and kisses his cheek, and I see that she's making him uncomfortable, but she doesn't seem to notice. "How has your day been, sweetums?"

"Fine, fine," he says as she releases him. "I was just coming to check on Rose. How are you today? The king is asking."

"Oh, uh… fine," I tell him, wondering if I should fill the Beta in on the accident with the dress. After all, it sounds like Miss Emily will be telling King Gene everything shortly anyway.

"Emily came around the corner with a glass of wine in her hand and spilled it all over herself and blamed Rose," Shelby says, putting her hands on her hips. "Really, who carries around a glass of wine with them wherever they go? It's not even noon yet! And then she screamed at her and threw a fit at the maid who came to clean it up as well. The nerve of that woman!"

"Keep your voice down, dear," Adam says, holding up his hands in front of his wife. "There's no need to let everyone know you're displeased with the king's cousin."

"Why shouldn't I be?" she asks in an even louder voice. I get the impression Shelby doesn't like to be shushed. "She's just terrible!"

"I understand your feelings, dear, but she's still the king's cousin," Adam reminds her.

"So what?" Shelby asks, her eyes huge. "Are you taking her side?"

"No, dear," he says, and I get the idea that perhaps the happy couple is not as happy as they first appeared. But I feel very uncomfortable standing here as they continue to argue.

I think I see my room up ahead. I'm not quite clear which one is which, but I vaguely remember the vase of flowers by the door. I dismiss myself and say, "I'm going to lie down for a bit." Neither of them seems to notice.

Somehow, I manage to guess right and walk into my room, but there will be no lying down. A spread of food awaits me, and the maids who have just finished setting it up grin from ear to ear. "Your lunch is served, Miss Rose," one of them, a blonde with a button nose and big hazel eyes, says.

"Why… thank you," I say, looking at all of the food. There are enough sandwiches on the table to feed the entire army, and I can't even count how many different kinds of fruit there are. I haven't ever had a lunch like this in my whole life.

"You're welcome, my lady," the other girl, a tall, dark girl with satiny skin and a wide smile says.

They are both beautiful, and I feel myself thinking maybe under different circumstances the three of us could be friends, but Shelby mentioned earlier, while she was babbling on, that I should try not to treat the maids as my equals.

The only problem is, under my circumstances as the only Breeder, I don't think anyone here is my equal.

I sit down to eat, but I haven't made it very far into my first sandwich when my door flies open, and Shelby comes in—crying.

I've never had to comfort a friend when she's fought with her husband before because I really don't have that many friends, so I don't know what to say, but when Shelby flings herself at me, I wrap my arms around her and pat her back.

I'm getting the impression that everything here at the castle is not what it seems.

CHAPTER 10: SCHEMES

Emily

"That stupid bitch!" I mutter to myself as I head back to my room to change clothes.

Martha and Beatrix are right behind me, agreeing with my every word, as well they should, but there's nothing they can say to make me feel better.

I know who the girl was. Hell, the entire kingdom knows. I was there when she was presented to everyone. I stood in the back, near the four Alphas, my four Alphas, at least, that's how I liked to think of them. This stupid bitch probably thinks of them as hers.

I can't wait to see her face when she finds out how fucking wrong she is!

Back in my room, I find another gown and change into it quickly, downing another glass of wine before I leave the room. I'm late now, and my cousin, King Gene will not appreciate that. But I'll just tell him the truth: that stupid little twit of his got in my damn way.

"All right," I tell the others, checking myself out in a full-length mirror one more time. I look great, of course, I do, but I don't like this red number as much as I liked the other one. "Let's go."

"Yes, Emily," Martha says with a grin. "You look lovely."

"Maybe we'll see one or more of the Alphas along the way," Beatrix adds with a grin.

"Maybe we will," I tell her, "but I can guarantee you, even if we do, none of them will pay you any mind. You look like a big poofy cloud in that stupid dress!" I see her face crumble and I turn away to cover my laugh. Some people say I am cruel for being so honest, but I don't give a damn what anyone thinks.

I know why these two are here. They pretend to be my friends because I have power, but they really just want my leftovers. I understand that. I would probably do something similar if I was ugly and had no connections.

Even though their fathers are powerful Deltas in my pack, they're really no ones in the big scheme of things. Back home, they're used to having their asses kissed, but not by me. And at the castle, they are no ones with a capital N.

I head back down the hallway, making sure to steer clear of that klutzy bitch, and make it to my cousin's office about half an hour later. His assistant, a tall, thin reed of a man named Thomas, is standing outside of his office.

I wonder where his secretary, Eleanor, is. That old cunt always makes me want to smack her in the face every time I see her. She thinks she can talk to me like I'm an ordinary citizen, and I hate her for it. But Thomas is putty in my hand.

"Ah, Miss Emily," he says with a nod. "The king was just asking for you."

"Yes, I'm sure he was. I'm late because that stupid bitch Breeder spilled wine all over my dress."

"I will let him know," Thomas says, stepping back into the office. He's allowed to do that, which I guess makes him feel pretty special.

He's back a moment later, and he holds the door open for me. Martha and Beatrix sit down in chairs in the hallway, waiting for me. I see that Martha is still dabbing at her eyes, and I can't help but chuckle under my breath.

"Emily!" my cousin says as I walk in. He stands and I go around the desk to hug him and air kiss both cheeks. "You look lovely. Thomas told me about your accident. Are you alright?"

"I'm fine, darling," I tell him, sitting down across from his desk. "That girl is… something else."

"Yes, I wonder why she thought it necessary to be drinking so early in the morning," he says, shaking his head.

I don't correct him. "Well, coming from her miserable little pack, perhaps that's the only way she can make it through the day," I supply, glad I didn't bring my wine glass in with me. I rarely have it out of my hand, but since I am a shifter, it's difficult to make me drunk. It's not like I'm a frail little human who gets affected easily by alcohol.

"Well, I'm glad you're here now," he says with a wide smile. "How are you liking the castle?"

"It's wonderful," I tell him. "I'm really enjoying my time here. I will be happy when that Breeder's job is over with though. She's not very pleasant." I wrinkle my nose.

"Is that so?" he asked. "Beta Adam was telling me earlier that his wife, Shelby, thinks the girl is a delight."

My face creases further. "Oh, dear King Gene, my cousin, my darling, that Shelby is something else as well. I'm afraid she's not quite sophisticated enough as a lady to know what she's speaking about. But… I suppose they are both fine in their way. They can't help their backgrounds." I can tell my cousin must like this awful Shelby girl, so I scale it down a bit.

"Yes, indeed," he says. "Well… if you're not going to be friends with them, at least you will be able to get along. Assuming there are no more incidents."

"Indeed," I say with a smile. "Perhaps I can even help them a bit. Shelby will be here for the long term, so she should know a bit more about being a proper lady. As for the Breeder, well, maybe she can return to her own pack a little more… polished."

I don't intend to help anyone with anything, but I want my cousin to think that I'm capable of being helpful.

The only thing I can guarantee him for certain is that there will be further incidents. I just can't help myself! I love to see people like that Breeder girl squirm when they know they are in trouble.

It would be a shame if the Alphas all decided she was reprehensible. But then… I suppose I'd rather have her get all fat and pregnant, rather than me. I've never cared to have a child. Let her do all of that, and I'll just stick around to reap the benefits.

"Have you met the Alphas yet?" King Gene asks me.

I shake my head. "No, sadly I have not. I believe I saw them at the announcement yesterday, but formally, no we have not met. Perhaps we could have a ball?" I say, clapping my hands together. I do love a party.

"A ball?" he repeats. "That's an interesting idea. Possibly… later on. Right now, they are all busy getting to know the girl. They don't know about you yet, dear. We'll save that for a later time."

I nod. I already know that. But it wouldn't hurt to have them aware of my existence.

I don't need my cousin's help with that, though. I've always been quite good at helping people to notice me.

"Well, I am here and ready to do whatever you'd have me do, darling," I tell him. "My father always said you were his favorite cousin, even before you claimed the throne.

Now, I must agree. It's so lovely to be here in the castle and to finally have a chance to know you better."

King Gene smiles at me. My charm is working overtime, which is good because every word that comes out of my mouth is a string of lies.

"Thank you, Emily," he says. "I'm so pleased you're here and that our plan was agreeable to you. I have no doubt you are the perfect woman for the job."

I smile as he stands and comes around the desk. Realizing our discussion is done, I rise and wrap my arms around him. "I'm so pleased you thought of me."

He kisses my cheek. "Who else could I possibly choose for such an important job?"

With confidence, I tell him, "No one, cousin. I am the perfect woman for this position, and I will not let you down."

He kisses my cheek again, and I begin to wonder if he's forgotten we are cousins. Oh, well. We are distant cousins, after all. May as well let him get his jollies.

When he's done kissing me, I twirl around and head out the door, feeling his eyes on my backside. I can't blame him. I have a nice ass. All men watch me walk away.

I head out into the hallway to collect my bitches and then head back toward the area of the castle where I'm fairly certain I can find an Alpha or two. I may not be able to pounce on them just yet, but that won't stop me from getting to know them and making sure they have their eyes on me.

When my work is done, all four of them will only have eyes for me.

That other bitch can pack her bags and go back home—right after she pops out that baby.

Poor ugly, fat fuck.

CHAPTER 11: THE MAN WHO WILL CLAIM MY VIRGINITY

"Miss Rose? It's time to get up."

I hear Vienna's soft voice next to me, but I don't want to open my eyes. It took me forever to fall asleep the night before, and now that I am in dreamland, I don't want to leave. It doesn't matter that I can't even remember what I was dreaming about.

"Miss Rose? The race will start soon!" she repeats.

"Race?" I ask. "What race?" My eyes open, and I blink up at her. This bed is way too comfortable. I never had this kind of trouble waking up back at home.

"The race the four Alphas are having, my lady," she relays. "The race to decide who will... be your first." Her cheeks turn red, and I realize what she is implying.

"Oh," I say, sitting bolt upright. "That race."

She nods. "Yes, that race, my lady."

All of this "my lady" business is so strange to me. It's giving me a headache. "Okay," I say as I roll out of bed. "I'm up." There was no point delaying the inevitable.

I head to the bathroom to take a shower while she gets my outfit ready, but I lock the door. It's not that I don't trust Vienna not to walk in on me while I'm showering. Actually, it's Shelby I'm more concerned about.

It's a little harder to hide in the shower than the bathtub. I can imagine Shelby pressing her face against the glass and trying to talk to me while I'm washing my armpits. I'd rather just keep the door locked to be safe against any perverts walking the halls here.

The day before, Shelby had been so upset about Beta Adam. But then… he had come by later and brought her flowers, and then everything was well with the world.

Relationships are complicated….

And I'm about to have four.

At the same time.

I finish showering and wrap a towel around myself. As I walk out, I see a nice outfit laid out on the bed for me. It's a pair of white, wide-legged slacks and a coral-colored tunic with one wide strap and nothing on the other side; it will sit on one shoulder while the other is bare.

"What do you think, my lady?" Vienna asks. "Is the outfit I've selected to your liking?"

"It's beautiful," I tell her. "But you can call me Rose. Really." Her eyes widen, like I am saying something unheard of. I have a feeling she won't take the note.

Rather than letting her dress me, I take the clothes into the bathroom and change. When I come back out, she styles my hair while another maid puts my shoes on me–gold strappy sandals.

Apparently, 'ladies' can't bend at the waist.

I also have my makeup done and jewels added to my ears, neck, and wrist.

I feel like a proper lady now.

But when I look in the mirror, I still just see me. The words that other woman had shouted at me yesterday, about my nose, come back to me. I wish I could hide my nose somehow….

I wonder if she will be there.

I'll find out soon enough.

A knock on my door lets me know my escort is here. Vienna opens the door to reveal a way too happy Shelby with her husband. "Are you ready?" she asks me.

I finish off a piece of fruit from the breakfast platter I was brought and nod. "I'm ready." Ready or not, I have no choice.

"You look beautiful!" she gushes, hugging me.

"Thank you. So do you." She waves me off, but honestly, she does look super cute in a yellow sundress.

"Let's go," Adam declares. "We don't want to be late."

Shelby rolls her eyes, and we walk out.

We wind down the long hallways and out a different door than I've been through before. Out in the woods, I hear a congregation of voices. Apparently, the majority of the people who live in the castle will be here.

I see the king seated on a throne-like chair, and Adam is walking me right to him, to an empty chair to his right.

King Gene remains seated as he greets, "Good morning, Rose."

"Good morning, Your Majesty." I bow to him, and Adam gestures for me to sit. He takes his place on the other side of him, and the chatter continues until we all see movement off to the north.

Four figures are walking toward us, followed by other men behind them, and I realize the four in front are the Alphas, and the ones trailing them are their Betas and other servants.

The four of them are only wearing short, tight, athletic shorts, and my heart starts beating out of my chest just looking at them.

When the four men come to stand in front of the king, I can hardly keep my eyes on their faces, not because I want to stare at their chests, although that is also the case. I'm just too nervous to make eye contact.

With everyone else quiet, the king begins to speak. "Good morning, Alphas."

"Good morning, Your Majesty," they all four say at the same time. I catch the eye of the man I saw in the garden the day before, and he winks at me.

Feeling my cheeks heat up, I drop my eyes.

The king doesn't seem to notice. "As you know, the winner of this race will determine who will lay with the lady, Miss Rose, first. In fact, the order in which you finish will determine the order in which the four of you have an opportunity to lay with her."

Again, my face begins to flame. The entire crowd can hear him and knows that I will be having sex with all four of these men. It feels like everyone is undressing me mentally as the king speaks and they imagine the pornographic scene. It makes me feel so dirty.

While some might be envious of me, others would probably think I was some sort of wanton whore.

King Gene finishes giving the directions, but I don't even pay attention. I just look at the ground in front of me.

I gather the gist of it, though. Whoever comes in first will get first dibs on me, and so on and so forth. The king said he trusted all of them not to cheat, but he wouldn't be monitoring the race track, which was a two-mile loop through the woods. Whoever gets back to him first will be the winner.

It is as simple as that.

The king gives the signal, and the four Alphas, who had already gotten into position, start running, leaping into the air and shifting mid-leap. I watch in amazement as their rippled, muscular bodies take on their wolf forms.

Of course, I am used to seeing people shift, but seeing such fine specimens of men turn into equally majestic wolves is pretty amazing.

Personally, I have never shifted. We just don't shift a lot at my pack, and I needed my hands most of the time—to shovel up waste and the like. I'm not even sure I'm capable of it yet.

I quickly lose track of who was standing where, so I'm not sure which wolf is which. They are all different colors, and even though sometimes a shifter's hair color will transfer to their fur, I am not sure if that is the case with these Alphas.

One of the wolves is a lighter color, so I think that might coincide with Mark's blond hair. One is red, so that might be Eli. The darker gray-colored wolf could be Reece since his hair is the darkest, but Tristan's hair is also dark.....

In all honesty, I could be wrong about all of them.

And then, it really doesn't matter to me who wins anyway. It's not as if any of them seem any better than the others when it comes to who I want to sleep with first.

Although, I do have to admit that Eli seemed really nice to me when I first met him.... Maybe he would be the most gentle, thoughtful.

But I have no idea which one will give me the best experience. So I will leave that, like all things, up to the Moon Goddess.

It doesn't take long at all for the crowd to go crazy cheering, and I realize that the wolves are coming into view around the edge of the loop.

It is so close, I can't tell who is winning. The four of them are all basically in one line across in a row. I see that there is a camera placed at the finish line, so we may actually need to have a photo finish.

"I bet all of them are running as slowly as possible," I hear a familiar voice snarl behind me. I don't have to turn my head to know who it is. It's Emily. "They probably want to come in last—or die on the way so they don't have to fuck that ugly bitch."

Fighting the urge to turn and look at her, as her friends burst into laughter, I keep my head pointed straight ahead.

She's just jealous she isn't getting any action.

The red wolf surges ahead, but then, one of the darker wolves charges forward, lunging just a bit ahead of him. Then it's the other dark wolf ahead by just a few steps, with the blond hanging back just a bit.

As the finish line comes into view, they all pick up speed, and to the naked eye, it's impossible to tell who finishes first.

Everyone leaps out of their seats or into the air if they are standing, clapping their hands and cheering.

"We have a winner!" the king announces.

The moment of truth: which Alpha will be taking my virginity?

CHAPTER 12: WHO WILL BE MY FIRST?

In the chaos after the race, I learn nothing. I have no idea who the winner is. I don't know the order the Alphas have finished, and no one can tell me what is happening.

Alpha King Gene claps his hands frantically, clearly happy with the outcome, though I don't know what it is.

How does he know? Maybe he doesn't care either.

He stands to congratulate all four of the Alphas, who are still in their wolf forms, on a great race and then says, "Thank you, everyone, for coming out!" and the crowd begins to disperse.

I stand, dumbfounded, still at a loss for words.

What is happening??

"Well, that was exciting!" Shelby says, grabbing hold of my arm. "To think, they all finished within one second of one another! They must have all been trying so hard to win!"

I think of what that other girl said behind me. Or trying really hard to lose….

Shelby leads me back toward the castle, but there's such a crowd around us, and I feel stupid telling her I don't know who the winner is.

I still can't figure out how everyone else seems to know.

As we walk back to the castle, I hear some villagers discussing it. "I swear, it was Alpha Tristan!" the man says.

"No, no, he was a full step behind Alpha Eli!" his wife protests.

So perhaps I am not the only one in the dark.

Shelby is chattering on about the clothes everyone else is wearing, mentioning names of people I don't know. "Gladys looked nice in that pink dress, but her hair was a mess. And then there was Syble. What was she thinking? White shoes? It's way past Workers' Day."

I nod, hoping we get a chance to be alone for me to ask her what is happening, but the crowds are busy with servants scurrying around, in a rush to prepare for… something.

I don't get a chance to ask her before we reach my room, and then, as we are standing at the door, she says, "Well, I have to go. I'll be back later, though."

"But–" I stammer.

"I'm sorry," she says. "It's just… I have to go help Adam with preparations for dinner tonight. He hates that sort of thing." She rolls her eyes.

"Dinner?" I repeat.

"Yes, you're having dinner with the king and all of the Alphas. And then… well, I suppose you'll find out what your first man's plans are." She winks at me, and I feel my stomach tighten up.

Could I be expected to sleep with one of these Alphas tonight?

I don't even know who won!

"But Shelby," I protest.

"Don't worry. I know he looks intimidating, but he's very sweet. He'll take care of you." She smiles reassuringly at me and takes a few steps away.

"Who?" I ask her.

She laughs. "Very funny, Rose. As if you're not all in a tizzy over this. I know I would be." She mouths, "He's hot!" and spins around to leave.

Sighing, I walk into my room. Vienna is there, waiting for me, her eyes wide. "Who won?" she asks me.

"I don't know!" I fall face-first into the bed.

"Miss Rose, if you don't wish to tell me, that's fine. I was only wondering what shade of gown to put you in for the dinner."

I grumble into the bedspread. "I really don't know!"

"What?" she asks.

Flopping over like a fish out of water, I explain. "The race was very close, and everyone leaped up in front of the finish line. I honestly don't know how anyone knows who won!"

She smiles at me. "Well, we will just have to go with a neutral color, then, one not associated with any of the packs."

"The packs have colors?" I ask reticently, worried about sounding ignorant.

"No, but the Alphas have favorites. It's fine."

"How do you know the Alphas' favorite colors?" I can't help but ask.

She shrugs. "It's part of my job. I know their favorite scents as well." Her smile is bright, and she seems proud of herself. As she should be.

I have several hours before I have to get ready for dinner, so I spend much of the day trying to occupy my mind. I don't want to think about the Alphas, and I don't want to think about my family.

Here, I have time to read, which is something I always enjoyed at home but never had a spare minute for, so I curl up in a chair and lose myself in a book. I decide on a steamy romance I found on the bookshelf. It makes sense that I would read that. Perhaps I will find some tips.

It's all rather explicit, though, and by the time I'm through the second sex scene, my face is red, my heart is pounding, and I'm thinking, "I can never do that!"

But I read on. This is my future!

At about 5:00 in the evening, Vienna suggests I go take a bath. She runs the tub for me, and eventually, I go in, locking the door behind me in case Shelby shows back up.

While I am in there, alone, I make a little inspection of my own parts. I'm not sure I have all of the nubs and buds and whatnot I've read about in the book. I feel grossly uninformed when it comes to my own anatomy.

When I get out of the tub, I am not any more prepared than I was going in.

But Vienna gets me all made up in a beautiful silver gown. She and a few other maids come in to do my hair and makeup. I look really pretty–for me–and the maids are all kind enough to tell me how "ravishing" and "gorgeous" I am. I wonder if I will get any food stuck in the gap between my teeth or if my nose will get in the way when the Alpha tries to kiss me.

A couple of hours after the preparations begin, there's a knock at the door. My breath catches in my throat. Time sure has flown by. Is it really so late in the day already?

What if it's him? What if it's my Alpha?

Vienna pulls the door open to reveal Beta Adam. "Good evening, Miss Rose," he says. "I'm here to escort you to dinner."

"Oh," I say, trying not to sound disappointed. "Where's Shelby?"

"She's… late," he says, closing his eyes.

"Okay," I say, not wanting to poke the bear.

"I didn't want you to be late, too."

I can only assume they've argued about this before he left her to come get me.

"Well, I'm ready," I say. I lift my gown with both hands as I walk toward him, afraid I might otherwise trip.

Beta Adam takes my arm, and the two of us walk in silence to the dining hall. I am certainly not asking him any questions about the Alpha. He doesn't seem like a chit-chatty kind of guy.

When we arrive, Adam pulls a chair out for me on one side of the king. His Majesty greets me, and I try to keep my heart from beating out of my chest. I am near the center of a huge table where hardly anyone else is sitting. Yet.

Adam leaves, I presume to go back and get his wife.

A few minutes later, more people begin to pour in, and my eyes fall on the handsome face of the blond Alpha–Mark–as he pulls out the chair next to me.

"Good evening, Miss Rose," he says to me after he has already greeted the king.

"Hello," I say. I can hardly get the word out.

The rest of the guests come streaming in, and almost immediately, someone says to Mark, "Congrats on winning the race Alpha," and I bite back my shock.

He is the winner!

That means, the handsome man sitting next to me gets to claim me first…. My hand trembles as I pick up my fork to start the first course.

The other Alphas are seated right across from me, so I could speak to all of them–if I could speak at all. But I remain quiet for most of the meal because no words will come out of my mouth no matter how hard I try to force them. I am too nervous.

Besides, on the other side of King Gene, Beta Adam, and Shelby, sits Emily, the king's cousin, and she will not stop talking.

She and I are going to continue to have major issues.

"You look so handsome tonight, Eli," Emily says seductively. I can't see her, but I see how the Alpha responds.

"Why thank you, Emily," Alpha Eli says, smiling at her politely.

Kelly, who is sitting right next to her brother, looks almost as annoyed as I do. I remember how much I liked that girl when I first met her.

As dinner goes on, Mark tries to speak to me, but all I can give him is a bunch of one-word answers.

"How do you like it here?" he asks me.

"Fine," I say, not lifting my face to look at him.

"Do you miss your family?" he wants to know.

"No," I say. It's true, but he might think I'm not a nice person.

"You're not close to your parents?" he inquires.

"No." Is that the only word I'm capable of speaking?

He nods his head. "Me neither," he says, and it's nice to know I'm not alone.

Rather than asking me questions, he begins to talk about his life back at Rapids pack. I'd much rather listen to his smooth voice than try to talk to him.

Dessert is delivered too quickly. He tells me about his younger brother while I poke at my cake, and then, when the plates are taken up, he says, "Are you ready to get out of here?" and flashes me a dazzling smile.

I can't say no, but my heart is beating out of my chest as I look at him and slowly nod.

I can't believe the moment is here–and I'm about to give my virginity to a man I've just met! My hands continue to shake as I prepare to stand.

His smile widens. "Great. I thought I'd never get you alone."

He gets up and takes my hand, and we say goodnight to the king. We back away from the king and then, nearing the door, as we turn to walk away, I see Emily glaring at me. She lifts a hand and rubs her nose, and I feel my insides begin to scramble.

All I can think about is… what if my giant nose gets in the way?

CHAPTER 13: KISSED BY AN ALPHA

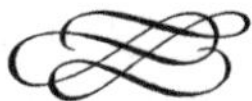

As Mark walks me out of the dining hall, amidst several other couples who are also leaving, I can't help but raise my free hand to my nose.

That Emily is awful! Why did she have to do that? Pointing at her nose to remind me that mine is too big?

"Is everything all right?" Mark asks me, concerned.

"Oh, yeah," I say, smiling at him and pulling my hand away. "I'm just… uh… itchy."

His eyebrows knit together. "Are you okay? Allergies?"

"I'm fine," I tell him. I want to do more to reassure him, but I can't even think of what to say.

"Well," he adds, "I was going to ask if you wanted to join me in the garden for a bit before we, uh, come back inside… but I don't want you to be uncomfortable if you're allergic to something outside. Or is it a food allergy?"

"Cats," I blurt out. "I'm allergic to cats."

He slows his pace and turns to look at me, not any less confused than he was to begin with. "But… there were no cats at dinner."

Of course, he has a point.

I stammer, my mouth moving, but nothing coming out, when he continues. "Although, that chicken dish was a little questionable." He laughs, and I do, too, though I don't get it at first.

When I finally do, I laugh harder. Is he implying that the chicken meat was really cat?

By the time I can speak again, I put forth the idea, "I think someone I was sitting next to has a cat at home."

"That makes sense," he agrees, taking me down a side hall and out the door. Whether or not he truly believes me is a whole different question.

The sky above us is ablaze with bright stars that make the moon look dimmer than usual and lend a purple tinge to the rest of the darkness between their twinkling lights. I gasp at how beautiful it is out here, and Mark pauses, holding my hand, and confesses, "It's beautiful, but it's not the most beautiful sight I've seen tonight."

I look at him, my eyebrows raised, thinking he means the flowers in front of us, but then, when his cheeks tinge a slight shade of pink, I realize he means me.

"Oh… thank you," I say, my eyes larger than the saucers from dinner.

He is charming. It's almost like he means it.

Mark keeps his fingers wrapped around mine as we stroll through the garden, smelling the flowers, and gazing at the fountains. This is a different garden than the one I was in the other day, and around every corner, there seems to be another lovely sight that takes my breath away.

"Were you pleased when you won?" he asks me as we sit down on a bench near a fountain depicting a howling wolf gazing up at a full moon.

I am surprised by his question, and I don't know how to answer it. "Uhm… I was surprised," I tell him.

"Yeah, me, too," he admits, and once again confusion washes over me. He was surprised I won? "I have never thought I was particularly fast. I'm a good fighter, but this was a race. So I didn't expect to win. When they showed us the photo finish, and I was slightly ahead of the others, I was shocked." He gives me a humble smile, and I feel my heart warm.

He is not quite who I thought he would be, based on my first impression of him. I just assumed that someone who looks like him is probably pretty stuck on themselves. But so far... he's been very humble.

"This whole situation is completely contrived, and that could make it very awkward," he says, reaching over and brushing a strand of hair away from my face. "I'm just glad that the winner is a sweet girl like you and not some... loud, pretentious brat who acts like none of us are good enough for her."

"Not good enough?" I echo. "Do you ever feel that way?"

He shrugs, the warmth from the brush of his fingertips still heats my cheek, and I don't want him to withdraw his hand. "Not usually. But some girls...." He stops talking and shakes his head.

Emily comes to mind. She would be that way, wouldn't she?

"Rose, if it were up to me, I'd take my time. I'd get to know you. I'd spend as much time as I can with you before... before I even attempted to see how compatible we might be in the bedroom. But... this is a different situation, and I honestly can't afford to let my chance go when there are three other guys that I know won't be as willing to take it slow."

My breath catches in my throat as I consider what he is saying. "I understand," I tell him.

"But I don't want to force you to do anything you're not ready for either." His voice is so soft and considerate, I can't help but place my hand on top of his where it lay on the bench between us.

"You're not," I assure him. "I'm... terrified." An uncomfortable giggle escapes my lips. "But I understand my duties as well. I can't let my pack down or the king."

"It sounds like we have similar allegiances, then," he says, his hand squeezing mine. "I don't take my responsibilities lightly."

"Neither do I," I affirm to him.

He nods and then, there in the moonlight, he leans over, and his lips brush against mine. His mouth is warm and soft. I envision this is what the brush of an angel's wings must feel like.

He lifts his hand to steady me, his thumb caressing my cheek as I feel my heart begin to pound in my chest. His kisses are slow and sweet, with no pressure at all, and when he does finally nudge my mouth open with his tongue, it's slow and simple.

And natural.

He tastes like mint, though I suppose I still taste like the cake I have just eaten. He doesn't seem to mind as he kisses me even deeper, and I find myself lifting a hand to place on his shoulder to keep from sliding off of the bench.

I have never kissed anyone before, so this is all new to me. New and… exhilarating.

After a few minutes, Mark puts some distance between us, leaving me breathless and wanting more. "Do you want to go inside?" he asks me. "I promise, I'll take my time. I don't want to hurt you."

I feel like my entire body is vibrating with adrenaline and fear, but I can also feel an ache between my legs like I've never felt before.

I believe I read about that in the romance novel….

Apparently, there's only one cure for that particular ailment, and it's currently tucked inside Mark's pants.

"Yes," I tell him, and his smile widens, his white teeth gleaming in the moonlight.

Without another word, he stands, taking my hand, and gently pulling me to my feet.

We walk inside, and I have to wonder if Emily will appear out of nowhere, dropping into the hallway to sabotage me. But she's nowhere to be found, and when Mark pushes open his bedroom door, I feel like my knees might give way.

Here we are, in his bedroom, dozens of candles lit around the room, with rose petals spread all over the dark blue satin bedspread.

He pauses next to the bed and gestures for me to sit down, which I do, trying not to let him know how unbelievably nervous I am.

Mark drops to his knees in front of me, and my heart begins to pound. Is he going to do that swirly thing I read about?

No, he's reaching for my shoes. He unbuckles them and slides them off, and I feel like I can breathe again. Then, he stands and carefully removes his jacket and his own shoes, tossing his suit jacket on the back of a chair before he sits down next to me on the bed.

Brushing my hair back again, he says softly, "Why don't we just go back to kissing and see how that goes, okay? That seemed to work well."

I nod, afraid to try to speak for fear nothing will come out.

He smiles at me and leans in. I hold still, afraid I might poke his eye out with my nose if I move too fast, and he kisses me over and over again, one hand on my waist, the other on my cheek.

Kissing him is delightful. It makes me feel like I am floating away, but when his hands begin to explore my body, I find myself breathless again.

I'm not sure I'm mentally ready for this!

My body seems to disagree with my conscious thought as I respond to him.

But… it's happening either way, so I may as well accept it.

Mark tugs at the zipper in the back of my dress, and I know I will have to stand up for him to get it off. He helps me to my feet, rising with me so that he doesn't have to stop kissing me. My dress pools on the ground around my legs, leaving me in the white lacy bra and panties Vienna picked out for me.

"You're so beautiful," Mark says, his eyes roaming me before he returns to kissing me.

In the book, the woman undressed the man, but I am too afraid to even loosen his tie. Mark takes care of that, pulling his tie off, and then he unbuttons his shirt and disposes of that as well.

Hesitantly, I place my hands on his chest, and I am immediately entranced by the feel of his muscles beneath my palms. He pulls me closer to him, his hands roaming the bare skin of my waist and hips. I feel that sensation deep within me growing as my head swims again.

Mark pulls back and looks at me, and I smile at him, which makes him smile in return. "Are you ready?" he asks me.

Am I ready for this?

I nod, and he reaches for the button on his pants.

Yes, I think I am.

CHAPTER 14: SLEEPING WITH MARK

Rose

"Are you ready?"

Mark had asked if I was ready for this, if I am ready to give him my virginity, and I assured him I am, even though I am so nervous, I don't even think I can speak.

He unbuttons his suit pants and pushes them down, stepping out of them, leaving him only in his black boxer briefs. The bulge in his pants has me gasping.

I'm not sure how I'm going to fit all of that in here....

I guess we will figure it out.

His mouth is back on mine as he carefully guides me to the bed, lying me down and then climbing on top of me. The blanket is turned down at the corner, but we are not beneath it, and I am worried about him seeing my naked body.

He trails his hand along my side and softly caresses my skin as he continues to kiss me deeper and deeper. The taste of mint fills my mouth, and the more his hands roam over me, the more intoxicated I become.

He is positioned next to me so that the top of his body is leaning over mine. His left hand finds my breast through my bra, and with his thumb, he rubs my most sensitive spot. I feel myself harden beneath his touch and let out a soft moan.

He lifts his head and looks into my eyes. "Does that feel good?" he asks me.

I feel my cheeks tinge with pink, but I decide I need to be honest and nod.

He smiles at me, as if I have just given him a reward for a job well done, and presses harder. I wonder if he will remove my bra, but so far, he isn't doing that.

Part of me wishes he would.

His mouth slides down to my neck, and his teeth nip my earlobe. His hand slides down my side to my hip, and then he places it between my legs on the outside of my panties.

I bite down on my bottom lip. His fingers are stroking me through the silky fabric, and it feels really good, but it makes me nervous. No one has ever touched me there before. I'm so wet, my body so ready for his, but what if he finds it funny that I'm responding this way?

"Goddess, Rose," Mark murmurs, "your body is so gorgeous, and you feel so good."

I don't know what to say, so I raise my hand to the back of his head and run my fingers through his hair, and he kisses me some more, each kiss measured and sweet, as if he is savoring the taste of me.

His fingers slip beneath the fabric of my panties, and he is touching me now. My breath catches in my throat at the feel of the contact in my most sensitive area.

"Are you all right?" he whispers.

"Yes," I murmur, and then his fingers are exploring my folds, and I feel my body moving in response, grinding against him.

When his finger first enters me, he is slow and gentle, and I moan again, my hips moving of their own accord.

"If I hurt you, let me know," he says, his warm breath fanning against my neck.

"Kay," I manage, but that's all I can get out because now he has two fingers inside of me, and he is thrusting his hand more quickly, stretching me slightly with each pass.

"Can I take your panties off?" he asks.

"Uhm-hmm," I tell him, longing for him to do just that.

Mark takes his fingers out of me and quickly strips off my panties. When his fingers reenter me, I welcome him. Without any restrictions, he can explore me even more deeply.

"You're so wet," he whispers. "You feel so good, and you smell like cantaloupe, my favorite." He smiles at me, and I feel a tingle of electricity all through my body.

My arms are wrapped around him, my fingers trailing up and down the muscle of his back, my eyes closed as I concentrate on how good he is making me feel. I find myself spreading my legs wider and wider, wanting more and more of him inside of me.

Mark pulls his mouth away from me, though his hand is still exploring me, driving me mad. "It's gonna hurt a little at first," he says, and as I look into his eyes, I can see concern. "I'm sorry about that. I don't want to be the one to hurt you. But after that... I promise, I'll make it feel good. Okay, Rose?"

"Yes, Alpha Mark," I say, my voice raspy with want.

He chuckles, his grin slightly crooked. "I think we are on a first name basis now, baby." He leans down and presses his lips to mine before he pulls away and slips off of the bed, releasing me for the first time since we began.

I try to catch my breath as I watch him. He slides his boxers down, and his thick cock springs free. He's so big... I can't help but stare. I've never even seen one of those before.

Mark is still smiling at me as he steps back over to the bed. "Do you want to touch it?" he asks me.

My eyes are wide as I stare at him, but I find myself saying, "No, that's okay."

"It won't bite," he promises.

I grin at him but shake my head. "Maybe next time."

That makes him smile wider, and I have to wonder if he is happy there will probably be a next time.

He climbs back onto the bed and positions himself between my legs. I feel a ball of nervous tension mounting in my stomach, but I trust him.

Mark leans down and brushes his hand across my face as he lowers himself onto me, and I feel him positioned outside of my entrance. "Rose," he says, a warm smile on his handsome face. "You're so beautiful. And sweet." He kisses me, softly at first, but then more intensely, as his cock presses against my entrance.

The deeper the kiss becomes, the more pressure I feel between my legs, and then, he thrusts inside of me. A sharp pain radiates through my core, but as he twists his hips and gently rocks against me, the pain dissipates.

And then… he is moving in and out of me, establishing a rhythm, and the pain is replaced by pleasure. Waves of euphoria wash over me as I respond to him. His tongue tangles with mine, and I wrap my arms around him, lifting my hips in response to his movements.

"Are you okay, Rose?" he whispers, locking eyes with me.

"Mmm hmm," is the only answer I can get out.

I never knew that my body could feel this good. My breath catches in my throat, and I find myself moaning and panting as my muscles contract and begin to spasm.

I've never experienced anything like this before, but whatever it is, Mark seems to like it because he is whispering, "That's it, baby, come for me, Rose."

Whatever it is he wants me to do, I have no control over what's happening to me, and I cry out again as an overwhelming sensation of warmth spreads throughout my tightened muscles.

A few moments later, while I am still trying to suck oxygen into my lungs, Mark speeds up his thrusting and grunts a few times before I feel his seed release inside of me. I hold on tightly to his muscular shoulders as he slows down and then rests his head on my shoulder, both of us struggling to breathe.

Mark's palm against my cheek grounds me as my heart rate begins to normalize. He kisses me gently next to my ear. "Are you okay, baby?" he asks me.

"I'm okay." I turn to look at him, and he smiles at me. He lifts himself out from between my legs and lies down next to me, pulling me against his chest.

It's over—I've done it, and when I look at Mark, I know, the Moon Goddess has had a hand in all of this.

I have no doubt, of all of the men in the world, Alpha Mark was the best choice to be here with me in this moment, and as he wraps the blanket around us, and I close my eyes, I can't imagine being with anyone else.

Ever.

CHAPTER 15: A BATTLE AT BREAKFAST

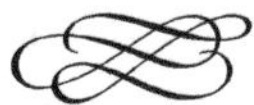

I don't want to walk into breakfast with the other Alphas.

I already know how this conversation is going to go.

If it were up to me, I would've continued to lay in bed with Rose all day, but she has a schedule to follow, and so do I. As I get ready to go to the room that the four of us have breakfast in… together… every day, I feel my heart hammering in my chest.

This is bizarre. We are sharing a woman! A beautiful, intelligent, sexy woman.

I straighten my tie and think about how amazing Rose felt. I am one lucky bastard to be the one who got to claim her virginity. No matter what happens in the contest, whether or not I impregnate her and become the next king, or I end up losing, no one will ever be able to take that memory from us, the night we shared together when she surrendered herself to me, and I was the first man to ever feel her body wrapped around his.

With a deep breath, I head down the hallway, hearing voices from behind the heavy wooden double doors as I approach. I have a feeling I am the last to arrive.

Walking in, I pause in the doorway as a hush falls over the other three Alphas. They are all staring at me, wide-eyed.

Waiting.

I clear my throat. "Good morning, gentlemen," I say, assuming my regular seat at the table. "What are we having today?" The castle chefs always serve us a ton of delicious food every morning, and I am starving.

Having sex always takes a lot out of me.

The others say nothing, only exchange glances. I know what they want, but I'm not going to be the first to volunteer it.

"Pancakes? Omelets?" No one answers. "Gosh, I hope it's not chicken." The urge to meow comes to mind, and I can't help but laugh.

"What the hell is so funny?" Reece asks.

"Oh, it's an inside joke," I tell them. "You would've had to be there."

"An inside joke between you… and Rose?" Tristan asks, and I can see in his eyes that he's jealous.

I shrug. "Well… yeah. Don't worry. You'll get your chance to impress her with your wit." I'm not smiling anymore. The realization that Tristan will be taking my place next to Rose in bed–inside Rose in bed–later today makes my stomach tighten.

I don't think I'm a fan of this arrangement.

He nods. "That's true. I will be getting my chance. Soon." He grins at me.

I swallow hard as a servant girl brings us huge plates of eggs, bacon, and biscuits. She smiles at each of us, her grin a bit seductive, but she's not that pretty, and we all ignore her. Even if she was pretty, all any of us can think about is Rose.

And this servant girl has a disproportionately large nose. None of us really like a girl with a giant schnoz.

"Well, I guess you're not going to tell us anything then?" Eli asks as he spreads his napkin in his lap.

Picking up my fork, I say, "What is there to tell? Don't worry, guys. It was all business. Rose is… a professional."

"Are you calling her a whore?!" Tristan's silverware clatters to his plate.

I roll my eyes as I attempt to disarm him. "Of course not," I dismiss. "I mean, she was very much aware that we were just... doing what we were asked to do. It's not like there was any... emotion involved."

"There wasn't?" Reece sounds surprised. "With you?"

"What's that supposed to mean?" I ask him, no longer interested in my food.

"Nothing," he assures me. "It's just... you're kind of an emotional guy by nature, Mark. You wear your heart on your sleeve."

"That's not true," I argue, and the other two laugh and nod in agreement with Reece. "Well, it doesn't matter," I tell them. "What's done is done, and now it's everyone else's turn." I force a smile to my face, but I'm sure it looks like a grimace.

"Well, I would thank you for passing the baton," Tristan begins, picking his fork back up, "but I wouldn't want anyone to be confused about which one of you I'm planning to sleep with tonight. I'll take the gorgeous blonde girl, thank you very much."

That got another laugh out of the others, and I chuckle a bit, too, just trying to seem normal. He wouldn't have to worry about touching my baton. That isn't how I swing.

But then... he will be touching Rose. Everywhere.

I stab a glob of eggs and raise them to my mouth, but even though I felt like I was dying of starvation a few minutes ago, now, I don't know how I'll manage to choke this down.

"So you're really not going to tell us anything?" Eli asks.

"Yeah, no pointers at all?" Tristan takes a drink of his orange juice. "You don't know what she likes or doesn't like?"

"Uh... I'm not sure I really feel comfortable talking to you guys about that sort of thing," I confess. "Just be gentle with her, and it'll be fine."

Tristan smirks at me. "Wait–are you serious? Be gentle. Dude, I'm not sure that's in my playbook."

I glare at him. "You'd better figure it out, man. She was a virgin up until a few hours ago, remember?"

Reece jumped in, agreeing with me. "You've gotta take it slow,

Tristan. Don't be trying any of your weird shit with her. Not right now."

Tristan's eyes bulge. "I don't know what you mean! Everyone I know likes that kind of stuff in the bedroom. If you're not using whips and chains, you're missing out."

"You'll just have to miss out this time then," Eli tells him as he runs a hand through his red hair, and I think he is probably afraid he might lose his temper. He is a ginger, and when he gets mad, it's hard for him to hide it.

"Fine! Fine!" Tristan says, raising both hands. "I'll be gentle with her. Jeez. Why don't you guys keep your dicks out of my bedroom, huh?"

"Ordinarily, I wouldn't be telling you what to do with your dick," Reece says, speaking for Eli and me as well. "But that's our girl you're talking about." He gestures at all four of us. "She's not just yours."

"So don't hurt her!" Eli shouts.

"I won't!" Tristan yells back. "Relax!"

The four of us go back to eating, dropping the subject of Rose, but I can't help but think about how awful it would be later that night, thinking about Tristan making love to her.

I want to be the only one with Rose, but I have to share her with these other three guys.

I've been with quite a few women in my twenty-five years, but I've never met anyone who affects me the way that she does.

The feeling is both exhilarating–and terrifying.

We finish breakfast before anyone speaks again. "You guys up for a game of basketball later?" Tristan asks.

"I've got some work to do," Eli replies. "I need to check in with the leader I left in charge back home."

"Me, too," I answer. It is really hard to run a pack from this sort of distance, but we have to figure out a way to make it work because our Betas have to be with us as well. I don't really trust the three guys I've left in charge not to screw everything up, but at least my mother, who is still an acting Luna, is there to help keep them on track.

"No problem," Tristan says. "Maybe after lunch?"

"Sure thing," Eli agrees as he gets up from the table.

"Yeah, catch you later," Reece says, also rising.

I want to take the opportunity while we are alone to threaten Tristan that if he hurts Rose, I'll mess him up.

But I keep my mouth shut. I have to remember she doesn't belong to me. And I have to hope she is strong enough to speak up for herself.

"See ya," I say to Tristan as I get up to go.

"Mark!" he shouts, getting up from the table to follow me. Tristan is a big guy, even bigger than me, and it takes him a few hurried steps to get all of that muscular girth over to me. "Are you mad, man?"

"No," I tell him, shaking my head. "I'm thrilled. I can't wait until you take Rose to your room and have your way with her. In fact, I can't wait to hear the full report in the morning over breakfast."

We take a few more steps before he says, "I can't help but think you're being sarcastic."

I bite back another snide remark. "Yes, Tristan. I am."

"Well, I'm sorry, man, but that's kind of how this goes. We've gotta be nice to one another. We are allies, after all. Besides, Rose probably wouldn't like it if we were fighting with one another all the time."

I want to tell him that he can't presume to know what Rose will like because he doesn't even know her. But I know he's right. She wouldn't like for us to argue.

"Okay," I say to him. "Just... be gentle with her."

He bows his head to me, like I am his Alpha, and I snarl. Now who is being sarcastic?

Tristan chuckles and pats me on the back before he ducks into his room, leaving me to walk to mine. My heart is heavy, and with every second that ticks by, I can't help but think I am already awfully attached to Rose. I've never felt like this before about anyone.

Am I falling in love?

CHAPTER 16: WAKING UP

ROSE

The room is deafeningly silent except for the rhythmic sound of my feet pattering on the floor as I walk around, lost in my thoughts.

I look up and see the luxurious bedroom, adorned with flowers in every nook and corner. It is an exquisite sight; I would normally find it romantic in any other context, but right now it is suffocating me.

The memories of last night's passion that had momentarily left me fully satisfied are now evoking doubts and second thoughts. Did I please him? That's all my mind can think about right now.

My thoughts are violently interrupted by the sound of the door opening swiftly. I turn around sharply and see Vienna making her way in with a tray of bath salts in hand.

She seems a bit startled to find me back in my bedroom, but I'm the one who should feel that way for being intruded upon.

"Good morning," she greets me.

Is that a grin I glimpse on her face? Will everyone be looking at me like this today? The whole palace knows that last night I had a tumble between the sheets with Alpha Mark. How much more awkward could all this get?

Bedroom affairs are meant to be private, and it seems unfair that my bedroom schedule is out for the whole world to observe.

"Good morning, Vienna," I say plainly as I turn my back to her. The mischievous leer on her face as she continues to gawk at me is making my face hot.

"I didn't know you were back from… you know… ahem…. well, I brought you some Himalayan bath salts. They are great for reducing inflammation and irritation. I thought they would be useful to you after last night."

I turn around in time to catch that naughty, lingering smirk on her face. Where did she think I'd be at this time? Sex wasn't supposed to last that long, was it? Did I do something wrong?

"Any salts there that could just make me disappear for the rest of the day today?"

Vienna blinks at me as she makes a funny sound and starts coughing. I can tell she is trying her hardest not to laugh. I am glad she finds this amusing. It slightly eases the awkwardness until I realize I'm the one she's laughing at, not with.

"My lady, forgive me for giggling. You don't look bad in any shape or form. I can tell you that most palace maids envy you and this opportunity you get with these handsome Alphas. Although after your bath, we are going to have to use a bit more concealer than usual."

I frown at that statement. I have never been one to need that much makeup. Why would I need it now? Had my first night with a man turned me into some sort of monster? Is that what happens when a woman gets with a man for the first time?

I rush to look at myself in the dressing table mirror. Has my nose grown bigger? Have my womb horns transferred to my face? Nowhere in those books had I read about transforming after giving up one's virginity.

As I look at my reflection, I see nothing amiss except for my hair, which looks all roughed up. Well, my hair couldn't be the cause of the need for concealer. A brush could easily fix that.

Vienna seems to sense my panic, and she walks over to me. She places the tray on the dressing table. "May I?" she asks as she lifts my hair, which is in a messy ponytail. My neck bare, she points at two huge red spots on my skin. I gasp.

Had there been mosquitoes in Alpha Mark's bedroom? How big had they been to cause such huge marks? My eyes meet Vienna's in the mirror. "It seems like Alpha Mark left his mark on you."

I bring my eyebrows together. What did she mean by 'mark'? Did one get marks after making love to wolves? No one had told me about this side effect. If I was going to be sleeping with four Alphas, and they all left marks on me, how would I look afterward?

I was definitely going to turn into a monster after all this. This is why I didn't think I wanted to be with any other Alphas after Mark. If I only stuck with him. At least all the marks would look the–

The voice inside my head is abruptly halted mid-sentence as a cheery laugh from behind us makes us both jump.

"Oh, my word! Last night seems to have been hot. Rose has a hickey or two!" Shelby says as she makes her way toward us.

Vienna bows her head slightly toward her. She hurriedly takes the tray and retreats to the bathroom.

I turn to face Shelby. She is smiling from ear to ear. "Spill! How was it?" Her eyes roam over me as she winks at me playfully.

Suddenly, I am again conscious of myself. Every inch of my skin has a highlighted sense of meandering anxiety, derived from the way everyone seems interested in my sex life. How much more embarrassing could this get?

Shelby pulls me to the bed, and we sit next to each other. I smile at her. Well, somehow I feel like I want to tell her all about last night. I want to hear her opinion and any advice she can give me.

Also, she needs to tell me more about these hickey marks one gets from having sex. I know I can't talk to anyone else about this. Not even my mother. Not that the woman is here. I haven't heard from my parents since I left. They must've gotten the money, though, or else they'd be calling.

Memories of last night flood my mind just as blood rushes to my cheeks. I blush and immediately feel embarrassed. Mark's face flashes in my mind. I can still feel the sensation of his pulsating rod inside me as my intimate muscles tightened around it, a wet pool beginning to form between my legs.

Shelby is watching me with pure fascination on her face. I can feel my face flushing. I raise a palm to my cheek and come to the realization that I am smiling like a love-struck puppy…. Well, maybe I am love-struck.

"That good, huh?" Shelby giggles.

I wish the ground would open up and swallow me right away. I haven't even said a word about last night, but my facial expressions seem to spill the tea hot and furious.

I nod in response to her question. "That good and more," I answer, and Shelby shrieks in delight.

"Well, I can see that." She points at my neck as affirmation.

"What is a hickey? Does it last forever? Do you get it from every sexual partner you encounter? I mean with four men leaving hickey marks on me…. I only have so much skin on my small body."

I can see a look of confusion on Shelby's face. She purses her lips as she watches me. I can see tears form in her eyes as she makes a funny sound in her throat.

Is she going to cry? What have I said? I wonder if she is trying to stop herself from breaking into sobs. Does she perhaps feel sorry for me getting these hickey marks from all these Alphas?

I nearly fall off the bed when Shelby burst out laughing. I look at her perplexed. What is so funny? Is this hickey mark thing common knowledge to every woman except me? Perhaps I should have tried to study more about these things. I probably sound very dumb right now.

Shelby's giggling dies down. She takes my hand in hers as she smiles at me. I can tell she is trying her best not to burst out laughing again.

"A hickey, my dear Rose, is a hot kiss a man gives a woman. The kiss burns with such passion it leaves a mark. Well, that and the sucking. It is also known as a love bite. It's just proof of the passion you shared with Alpha Mark last night, that's all."

I look at her intensely as more questions begin to formulate in my head. Was this a frequent occurrence then?

As if sensing my questions, she explains, "It is not something that happens all the time. Just once in a while, it can be thrown in during the waves of passion. If you don't get one, though, that doesn't mean there was a lack of passion."

I nod. I think I understand. I feel the corners of my mouth curving into a smile. Mark gave me a hickey.

Ah, for a newbie I should treat this as a medal for a job well done then. Why would I have to hide this under some concealer? I would love for Emily to see it. I smirk when I think of how she would react. It will surely wipe that stupid smug look she always wore.

I shake myself from my thoughts. I have more things I need to tell Shelby.

"I was so scared, but Alpha Mark was gentle. He made me feel like the most precious woman to ever walk the earth."

Shelby kicks her feet out of the sandals she is wearing and reorients her body to face me. She brings her feet up onto the bed. Now sitting cross-legged next to me, she bats her pretty eyelashes.

I giggle. She looks like a kindergartener getting comfortable for story time.

"How is he in bed? Is he as big as I assume he is? Did you lie on your back with your legs up afterward? It betters the chance of the seed reaching the egg."

I feel my face burn up. That is a very intimate question I didn't want to answer. Some secrets are best kept for my eyes and heart only. However, I will keep the 'lying on my back afterward' thing as handy advice for next time.

"I have nothing to compare him to," I remind her. "I was scared of spending the whole night with him," I confess, directing the conversation away from her prying question.

I am glad when she doesn't push the matter. Instead, she replies to my confession. "Why? Did you think he would eat you while sleeping?"

If by eat she meant to eat my... I shake my head. I can't believe I am now having such dirty thoughts. Well, Rose is surely no longer a virgin even in the head. I am a woman now. Mark's woman.

"Ha, I usually kick people out of the bed in their sleep. Wouldn't that be a major problem? To kick one of my suitors…." I unveiled one of my deepest secrets.

Shelby nods with a grin plastered across her face.

Then, I continue, "That's one of the reasons I could never go to slumber parties as a child. I once went to a sleepover at this girl's house when I was nine. I kicked not only her but everyone else who had come for the slumber party. When I woke up the next morning, I was alone in her big bed. Everyone else had decided it was safer to sleep on the floor. Imagine spending the morning with everyone complaining of painful ribs and giving me the dirty eye. I was mortified."

Shelby bursts out laughing again, and this time I join her.

"Hey, we all probably were kickers as children. But, you are an adult now. I am sure you grew out of that phase. In fact, you are a woman, as of last night." She winks at me, and I can't help but giggle.

Yes, she is right about me being a woman, but I am not so sure about the kicking part.

I shift on the bed, and my stomach growls in response. I am hungry. I didn't eat properly last night, and now my belly is yearning for its daily quota.

"You need to take a bath now and then have some breakfast. We still have a wonderful day ahead of us, before another eventful night."

My stomach drops. Partly because she is here, and I don't want her to be a spectator as I bathe, and more pressing, I really don't want to be with anyone else tonight. I want Mark.

My Mark.

CHAPTER 17: SO MANY DOUBTS

Vienna's eyes become shrewd, taking me in as though she's seeing me in a new light.

"You are glowing!" she says. I feel a warmth creep into my cheeks. I feel rejuvenated after my bath. It was a peaceful soak, and I had been relieved when Shelby had walked out of the room, allowing me to bathe in private. For once.

The soapy warm water seems to have made the hue in my skin radiate. The hickey marks on my neck appear to be brighter as well.

I wince and move my head back as Vienna brings a brush with concealer close to the marks. I don't want the marks covered. I want to broadcast them to the world. She looks down at me and smiles.

"I don't think there is a need for that," I say. I really am proud of my hickey marks. I can hear a faint groan coming from Vienna. It appears she doesn't quite agree with my decision.

"I think it is best if we cover them. The lunch buffet we have planned is going to host lots of people. It is bad enough that everyone already knows about your private affairs with the Alphas, but actually walking around with a hickey or two will only make matters more awkward."

I lick my lips as I regard Vienna through her reflection in the vanity mirror in front of me. I mean, the mark is special to me, but I think she has a point: walking around with this will just be a reminder to everyone about my position here to fuck four Alphas. I know this is probably a secret elation and win that I should keep to myself.

I nod my head at her. She smiles and proceeds to cover my love bites with a generous amount of concealer. When she is done, I take a look at myself. There is hardly any evidence of the marks that grace my neck. Now, all I have to cling to are the memories of the gentleness Mark had ravished me with. That reminder is enough to cause a warm feeling to surge inside my chest.

After all the maids leave the room, I walk over to the tray that has been placed on the bedside table. I lift the silver cover from one of the plates, and the aroma of freshly fried hash browns hits my nostrils. I feel my mouth salivating.

I sit on the edge of the bed, and without bothering to take a fork, I pick up some hash browns between my fingers and shove them into my mouth. Two slices of toast are on another saucer, and I take one with my other hand and sink my teeth into the crispy bread.

I close my eyes and relish in the moment of bliss. It's like I have never tasted toast before. This is plain old bread, yet it tastes like some aphrodisiac at this present moment. After clearing the food and fruit in most of the dishes on the tray, I wash it all down with a glass of pineapple juice.

I look down at my abdomen and chuckle. I look like I am already a few months pregnant. I know this isn't possible. I might not know much about getting pregnant, but I am sure one doesn't begin showing after one night. I just ate like a little pig. I enjoy eating without an audience because then I don't have to worry about etiquette.

I slump back onto the mattress and lie facing upward. The movement of the sun rays on the ceiling is mesmerizing.

"I think we are on a first name basis now, baby." Mark's words from last night echo in my mind. I smile. I, Rose, am his 'baby.' I giggle and

the sound resonates in the empty room. Should I perhaps find a pet name for him too?

'Sweetie?' I shake my head. That just sounds so cliché and old fashioned. I need something a bit unique. 'Love...?' That is just jumping into dangerous territories. This is simply a duty and not love.

I close my eyes as I feel a lump form in my throat. This is hard. How am I to share all this with him without actually developing any feelings for him? Is it easy for him to just go along with this 'duty' without developing any deeper emotions?

I struggle to take in a steadying breath. I think I am falling for Alpha Mark. This isn't good. It isn't part of this contract that I have to fulfill.

I feel my mind drift into the dimness.

It seems my eyes were closed for just a minute before I feel someone shaking me. "My lady, you have to get ready for lunch."

I blink at Vienna, trying to remember where I am. The light from outside is still shining with determined brightness. I must have drifted off to sleep.

"What time is it?" I ask her before adding groggily. "And I thought I told you to call me Rose."

She shifts her weight to her other foot, and I can tell that my constant prodding for her to call me by my given name is making her uncomfortable.

I get up and walk to the mirror. Well, whatever makeup they are using sure holds up quite well. All I need to do is run a brush through my hair and put a touch of lip gloss on my lips before going to the dining room for lunch.

After a little touch-up, I walk down the long hallway toward the dining room. I wonder where Shelby is. I suppose I will find her there.

When I walk into the dining room, everybody is already seated. I breathe in relief to see that none of the Alphas are around. It seems to be just a women's affair. However, I don't see Shelby among the occupants of the room.

As my eyes dart around the room, they land on Emily. She looks at me with pure disdain, but for some reason, I am not fazed. I meet her challenging eyes with my own unwavering stare. It seems like we are shooting silent daggers at each other with only our looks.

"Look who has decided to join us. If it isn't the little for-hire breeder."

Great, more belittling words. I don't expect any different. I am a nobody compared to her social class.

But, is it me or do the woman's lips continue to look like duck's lips each time she says a mean statement? IS she making that pose on purpose? If so, why isn't anyone telling her it just makes her look super silly?

Kelly waves at me from the left side of the table and pats the empty seat next to her. I smile and walk toward her. At least I won't have to feel like the unpopular kid in high school who isn't welcomed at anyone's table. I can sit with Eli's sister.

"Hey," she greets me as I settle next to her.

"Hi," I answer and return her smile.

"You look beautiful," she says, and I feel my cheeks begin to feel warm. Is this goddess really complementing poor old me? My smile grows wider.

"I hear Alpha Mark is in a sour mood today. He even refused to eat his breakfast. Seems like something took away his appetite. It surely must have been something quite disgusting for him to not even be able to stomach his food. Something about last night. I wonder what it is that could have gotten him so flustered. The poor Alpha."

I turn around to face the speaker. My eyes meet Emily's mocking gaze. I feel my chest tighten. What is she talking about? Who told her about Alpha Mark?

"How would you know that?" Kelly asks, echoing my very thoughts and questions.

"A maid overheard him talking to the other Alphas as they were having breakfast," Emily answers coolly.

Kelly tsks. "I thought you were intelligent and classy enough not to indulge in idle servant gossip."

Emily flips her hair back. "It's not idle gossip if it's true. I saw him earlier, and he looked really pale. When I asked him if he was okay, he told me that his stomach wasn't all right. He had been throwing up the little food he had been able to swallow. Said it was due to something he saw or tasted last night. I just wonder what it was that disgusted him so severely."

I know she is talking about my night with the Alpha. I have been under a very childish illusion that he actually enjoyed being with me last night.

How could I have been so wrong? I feel a warm hand covering mine. I turn to face Kelly, who is looking at me and shaking her head slightly. I can see she means to comfort me, but I can't help the pain that is now fizzing in my heart.

If Mark wasn't satisfied, why did he have to tell the whole world and not just tell me? I can feel hot tears burn my eyelids. I try to swallow the lump in my throat and keep myself from breaking down in sobs.

I can't and won't cry in front of Emily. She will not get that satisfaction.

"Excuse me," I say in a hoarse whisper to Kelly. I calmly push my chair back and quickly walk out of the dining room. As I reach the hallway, I feel a hot tear escape and roll down my cheek. I walk even faster toward my room.

When I reach my chambers, I walk in and slam the door closed before leaning my back against it and allowing the tears and raw emotion to pour out of me.

Alone at last.

Now, at least I have a silent space alone that I can think back to what I may have done wrong. After all, it was my first time, and I'm sure Mark has had quite the experience in the bedroom being such an important, attractive, kind-hearted man and all.

Suddenly, I feel a pair of hands grabbing my shoulders. I yelp and jump. What the... I try to blink the tears away, and I begin to see a blurry figure of a tall man in front of me.

"Are you okay, Rose?"

What was *HE* doing in my room?

CHAPTER 18: IF THAT'S THE BEST YOU CAN DO

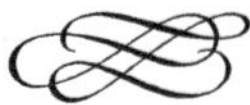

I am still sniffling as I look at Tristan, who is looking at me with readable worry in his eyes. I know I look like a hot mess, and I can feel some watery mucus dripping from my nose. I grimace as I can imagine what he is thinking seeing me in such a state. Why am I worried about what I look like in the supposed comfort and privacy of my room?

What is he doing in my bedroom? Didn't his mother teach him that girls' rooms are a no-no for boys? Do I need a privacy signpost on my door now?

My frustration with Emily and the blabbering Mark is turning into rage, and I am afraid if I don't get a grip on my emotions, I will take them out on Tristan. He is innocent... wait, scratch that. He is busy snooping in my room and thus is not innocent either.

"What are you doing in here, Alpha Tristan?" I try to be as polite as I can muster given the present circumstances and my somber mood.

"The door was unlocked.. I was looking for you. I'm sorry to have just come in. This probably makes me look like a person who doesn't respect boundaries, doesn't it?"

I wipe my nose with the back of my hand. 'You think?' I silently muse.

He reaches into the pockets of his jeans and takes out a small pack of facial tissues, handing it to me. My brow rises, but I accept the tissues. Does he always conveniently walk around with an unopened pack of tissues? Does he somehow always expect to meet a damsel in distress in need of tissues for her pathetic tears and snotty face—or are they for something else…?

"Thank you," I say as I open the plastic wrapping, taking one out and using it to dab at my face. What I really want to do is thoroughly wipe my face and noisily blow my nose, but I can't do that in front of Tristan. I have to try to act like a somewhat proper lady. Damn etiquette getting in the way.

"Why are you crying?" Tristan asks.

I shrug, not sure if I have the strength to begin explaining what is going on. I also don't think it's necessary to tell him about Mark's supposed nasty review of our night together. After all, if he told the other Alphas how horrible I am in bed, then I am sure Tristan already knows.

Maybe he is actually here to try to wriggle out of the inevitable disappointment that is sex with me. We don't want him projectile vomiting as well.

"Nothing. Just girl stuff."

I can see a crease form in his forehead. "Is it that time of the month?"

What the heck? I feel myself blushing from head to toe. Are none of these people shy about asking such intimate questions?

Having grown up in the kind of household I did, we never discussed such matters as if we were talking about some nice meal. To be standing in front of this Alpha talking about my period just felt so wrong.

"No!" I answer a bit louder than I mean to.

I side-step him and walk toward the bed, then remove my wedges and sit on the plush comforter. I look up and see him walk toward me.

He pulls out the chair from the dressing table and positions it in front of me before sitting down.

"Talk to me, Rose. Who made you cry? I promise I will deal with them personally."

I smile bitterly at him. Can he really straighten out the king's kin, Emily, by himself? And what benefit would it offer him?

His eyes have a genuine sincerity as they search mine. I feel myself warming up to this handsome room invader who keeps eyeing me with such concern.

"Since I got here, Emily has been taking incessant jabs at me. I mean, I know I am nowhere near as respected, beautiful, and well-connected as she is, but I don't think that gives her the right to bully me and stab me where it hurts the most every chance she gets."

I am surprised when Tristan throws his head back and lets out a belly laugh. I stare at him, shocked, wondering why he is making fun of me.

"My dear, Emily has nothing on you. She does all that because she is jealous of you," he playfully nudges my chin with his index finger. "If she had no relation to the king, I would use my last dime to put her on a spaceship to somewhere on another planet. Hell, I would pay extra to make it a one-way trip."

I can't help but laugh at his statement. He joins me and places his hand on my knee, the feel of it making me warm and fuzzy all over.

What is happening? Only Mark is supposed to make me feel like this, right?

"Thank you for trying to comfort me," I say as I tuck a stray strand of hair behind my ear while licking my lips that suddenly feel dry. I wish the lip gloss was as enduring as the makeup on my face.

"I hope I always manage to put a smile on your face. I don't think I can bear to see you sad or crying." I look at him, searching for a hint of humor in his features but realize that there is nothing but stern genuineness there.

My heart does a little spin and I know my skin must be resembling a tomato by now. This man is charming, protective, and kind. How had I not realized that before?

"Thank you, Alpha Tristan," I say, and I really mean it. I assumed he had come to find me to inform me of his intentions of dropping out of the race, but it appears the rumor that was allegedly spread about my poor bedroom prowess had not deterred him in the least.

"I do hope that, after tonight, you will drop that prefix. Maybe call me something else?"

My mouth is suddenly dry. I swallow hard. Is it him I am going to be with tonight?

"Uh… tonight be with me… I mean it is you I am on tonight," I stutter and trip on my own words. What the heck is wrong with me?

Tristan laughs and stands then comes to sit next to me on the bed. He pulls me to him, and my body complies. My head rests on the side of his chest. I can hear the faint sound of his heartbeat.

"Yes, my little flower. It is I you will be on tonight." Again he chuckles.

Oh, my! I am glad he can't see my face while sitting in this position, as I am sure by now I might be mistaken for a lobster.

"Oh, okay," I sigh and flinch. Is that all I have to say? Why can't I come up with something witty to say like those heroines I read about in those romance stories? Maybe I could have said something like, 'Yeah, my 'possum, I can't wait to really be on you!' Wait a minute, 'possum'? Where did that come from? Am I really this bad at giving pet names?

He gently releases me and claims my hand as he looks deep into my eyes. We are so close that I find myself praying that he can't hear how his closeness is causing my heartbeat to accelerate.

"Whenever anyone makes you sad, don't ever hesitate to come to me. You must know that these shoulders of mine are always there for you. I am here for you… my little precious flower. I will never allow anyone to hurt you!"

Precious flower? That's so much more endearing than a 'possum.

I nod. I can tell by his tone that he is serious. "Thank you," I respond gently.

He inclines his head to the side as if he expected me to say something more.

"I was hoping you would say, 'Thank you, sweetheart,' or whatever nickname you pick for me. But I understand I haven't earned that name yet. I promise, Rose, that I will work hard to please you and be deserving of that name."

Oh, wow. This man seems set on going all out to please wretched, poor me. If only he knew I was not good at returning the favor. I will need to do a bit more romance studying before tonight.

If I give him the best night, then he can tell that stupid Mark how great the sex was and how I blew him away. Is Tristan a kiss and tell kind of guy?

I nod and manage to squeeze his hand reassuringly.

"I can't wait," I release him excitedly, and I see him smile even with his eyes. He stands up with my hand still in his.

"Can I get a hug?" he asks, and I nod before standing. I have to stand on my tippy toes to embrace his neck. He pulls me closer to him and bends slightly to make my reach less strained.

I can feel his soft breath kissing the skin on my neck, and my breath catches. Like seriously, how am I having these butterflies for yet another man just after thinking I had fallen for Mark and had sworn I could never fall again?

"I hope you keep smiling, my little flower. Just know that I've got you, and you've got me. Tonight, I plan to spark magic into your existence. All I ask is for your permission to blow you away and make you scream my name, without the prefix. Please."

"You have my permission," I reply, wanting to add 'possum' to the end of it. My permission, my heroic 'possum' has a ring to it... I think.

I feel my body awaken to the prospect of tonight. His words carry both a promise and a threat...yet either way, I can't wait for our night together.

CHAPTER 19: TRISTAN IS A WILD MAN

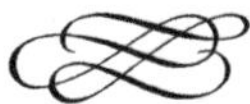

Rose

Nervous anticipation fills me as I wait for Tristan to arrive. Unlike last night with Mark, there's no dinner. There'll be no walk in the garden or anything romantic. He's just coming to my room.

To fuck me.

It isn't my choice for it to be this way, but Vienna informed me that this is the way it's going to be this time. Earlier, when she was getting me ready, she'd said, "Alpha Tristan sent a message earlier, while you were napping, that he'd be here around seven. He said for his 'little flower' to be ready for him.

Little flower... that is his nickname for me. I like it. I think it's a little old-fashioned, but nothing else about the broad-shouldered, muscular man screams traditional.

Now, I am sitting on the edge of the bed, wearing a light pink negligee under a matching silk robe, waiting for a knock on my door.

My heart is beating out of my chest.

Candlelight is all that illuminates my room—that and a few stray rays of moonlight that have made their way around the curtains. The old flowers had been replaced earlier in the day, so I can smell their sweet floral scent. I also smell like a flower garden, thanks to a second soak in the tub after my nap.

I am refreshed, but the nervousness is making me feel a bit ill.

I try to concentrate on how Tristan made me feel earlier in the day. He was so sweet. Maybe Mark wasn't so happy with my performance last night–I don't know, I still don't know who to believe–but I have a chance to please Tristan.

So I need to calm the hell down....

A loud knock on the door makes my heart stop. Before I can get the words, "Come in," out of my mouth, the door creaks open, and I see Tristan's familiar face staring in at me, his hair a bit disheveled.

A crooked smile crosses his face. "Hi there, little flower," he says. "Can I come in?"

"Of course." I not only find my voice, but I also get to my feet and step around the edge of the bed.

He is wearing a long black robe–and I think that's all.

I guess he didn't see the need to bother with pants, even in the hallway.

In his hand, he is holding a velvety blue box.

I come to a stop in front of him and can't help but smile. I have to tip my head back to look at him; he's so tall.

"This is for you."

He hands me the box, and I take it, but I don't know what to say. I'm shocked. I stare at it for a few moments before I ask, "Wh-what is it?"

"Open it," he says, chuckling deeply.

"Okay." I open the box to reveal a necklace. The chain is bright gold, and on the end of it dangles a golden encasement with a red flower in the center.

"It's a little flower," he explains.

"I see that," I tell him. "It's beautiful."

"Do you like it? I mean, really like it?" I can see hope in his eyes.

"I love it!" I tell him. "It's the most beautiful gift anyone has ever given me." I don't bother to tell him it's the only gift anyone has ever given me.

"Really?" His smile widens. "I made a special trip into the village to find it—well, something I thought worthy of your beauty."

I feel my cheeks flushing. I don't think anyone has ever complimented me like that either.

I tip my head up toward him to thank him again, but I don't get the words out because his mouth crashes down on mine. It takes my breath away, and I almost drop the box.

With his tongue still tangled around mine, Tristan takes the box from my hands and slowly walks me backward, placing it down on the chest at the base of my bed.

Then, his hands are on me, and he is pulling the tie around my robe so that it comes undone. His large hands are on my shoulders, pushing the smooth fabric down my arms to the floor.

When he finally pulls away from me so that I can take a breath, my lungs are burning. He is so much more intense than Mark....

Tristan grins at me and scoops me up, lifting me at my ribcage. I almost shriek in fear, but then he plops me down on the mattress and lets me go.

Using my elbows, I scoot back a bit, noticing the negligee I am wearing is so short; he can see my lacy, thin panties.

I guess it doesn't matter. He'll be seeing a lot more than that in a moment.

Standing across from me, he unties his own belt and quickly takes off his robe, tossing it across the room.

I was right. He isn't wearing anything underneath it.

His manhood is hard and at attention as he smiles at me, clearly proud of his... proportions. He should be; he's got a lot to work with, though I'm trying not to compare him to Mark.

Thank goodness I've already had a lesson on how to get so much man into such a tiny woman.

"Are you ready, my little flower?" he asks me, coming at me.

He pounces on me, his hands landing on either side of the bed near my elbows, his face hovering around mine, and his legs off to the side a bit.

I'm not sure how to answer that because I'm a little frightened, but I manage a nod before his mouth is devouring mine again.

Tristan isn't taking much time for foreplay. He seems eager to get on with it, and while I can respect that since this is a business arrangement, I just hope my body is as prepared as his is.

As he kisses me, his hands roam down my side, and he pulls my little nightie up out of the way, gliding his hand across my thigh to my crotch. My first instinct is to press my legs together, but I remind myself I belong to him tonight.

So I open up.

"Oh, yeah," he says, dropping his mouth to my neck. I imagine I am about to have a few more hickeys as his tongue trails along beneath my ear, and then his lips close, and he begins to suck.

He slides his fingers around the edge of my panties. "You're so wet and warm," he whispers into my shoulder, nipping at my skin with his teeth. A finger probes between my folds, and then deeper inside of me. "And tight," he adds.

It does feel good, and the more he kisses me, the more I feel myself loosening up.

His finger is joined by another, and then he uses both of them to press inside of me, as hard and fast as he can with my panties on. I find myself moving my hips in response.

"You like that, little flower?" he asks me. I have my eyes closed and am concentrating on how good he feels, so I don't respond. "You want more?"

He doesn't wait for an answer. Instead, he pulls his hand out and yanks my panties down, tossing them on the floor. Then he spreads my legs wider, and I can feel his eyes on me before his hand is there again, strumming me.

Three fingers now. I am gasping for air, feeling my muscles spasm around his hand, which makes him laugh with joy.

"Damn," he mutters. "I can't imagine how that's going to feel around my dick."

I slit my eyes to look at him, and I can see the excitement twinkling in his dark orbs.

Withdrawing his hand, he comes back up to me. I pant a few times, sucking in air, and then open my eyes to look at him. He is smiling down at me. "I'm going to try my best to be gentle with you, little flower, but if I get too rough, tell me, okay? I'm used to... girls that aren't anywhere close to being virgins who like a little pain with their pleasure."

My eyebrows lift. I know what it's like to have pain with pleasure because I just lost my virginity, but is he saying some women like that—all the time?

I don't have time to answer him because he has a hold of my nightie and is lifting it, so I sit up slightly, and it goes off over my head. Then, immediately, he moves between my legs, and his mouth clamps down on my left nipple, hard.

I whimper a bit, but he doesn't let go, and his hand is on my other breast, working my hardened peak like he thinks it's supposed to come off. It does feel good, but I'm so sensitive, it also hurts a little. I open my mouth to ask him to stop, but before I get the words out, he does.

His mouth is back on mine, and his hands are elsewhere, roaming, leaving trails of heat wherever they touch my flesh.

The tip of his cock has been at my entrance this entire time, but now, without warning, he thrusts inside of me.

"Ahh!" I cry out, the sudden fullness and stretching causing a shooting pain to spread throughout my core.

"Yeah, little flower," Tristan says. "You like that, huh?"

He must've mistaken my cry of pain as one of pleasure. I bite down on my bottom lip as he picks up speed. I didn't realize it was possible for anyone to do this any faster than he already was, but my Goddess! He reminds me of a jackhammer, he's thrusting his hips so hard and fast.

After a moment, it does feel good, though. He's hitting me in all of the right places, and with him going this fast, it feels like he is vibrating inside of me. Every time he makes contact with my most sensitive spots, I feel a wave of pleasure wash over me until I am gasping for air, and my toes start to curl.

My body goes into a spasm, and my muscles tighten. I try to cry out, but only gasps and moans come from my mouth. I dig my nails into his back and hold on for dear life….

Tristan doesn't let up, though. He continues at this frantic pace for what seems like hours, though I've lost all track of time, and I take short breaths whenever I can get a chance.

He seems like a tough man to please.

Finally, I feel him tightening up on top of me. He grunts loudly, and then his warmth spreads throughout me. He rolls off and collapses on the mattress next to me, breathing so heavily, it's as if he's just run an endurance race.

I remember what I was told about keeping my legs up, but at the moment, I can't even move.

We lie there next to one another, naked and glistening with perspiration, for several minutes before I feel his hand on top of mine on the mattress.

I turn to look at him. "Are you okay, little flower?" he asks breathily.

I nod, but no words can leave my lips. He grins at me, and as my muscles unclench and begin to relax, I notice a burning sensation… down there.

Yeah, I'm definitely going to be sore tomorrow, but I feel relief knowing that I left him satisfied.

"Maybe next time, we can get a little… wild," he says, grinning at me.

My eyebrows raise. Wilder than that? I can't imagine anything wilder than that.

Something tells me the man isn't bluffing.

CHAPTER 20: OR MAYBE HE'S A JERK

The other guys are likely hanging out in Eli's room. That's where we spend our evenings most of the time. I take a quick shower in my own chambers, get dressed, and then rush off to meet them. I can't help the huge grin that's on my face.

Rose is amazing–that was some of the best sex I've ever had in my life. And it was obvious she had an amazing time, too. She's so delicate and sweet. Getting to rock her world like that was a thrill, and I can't wait to share how awesome it was with the other Alphas.

I don't bother to knock because I can hear an action movie playing on the TV, and I hear Reece's voice, so I know Eli's not in there alone. I open the door and walk in, a triumphant smile on my face, my shoulders pushed back. I am the conquering hero.

"Tristan?" Eli asks, picking up the remote and turning the television down as I walk in and take my place in one of the chairs. "What are you doing here?"

"What do you mean?" I ask him. "I came to tell you all how fucking amazing that was!"

They exchange glances again, and I try to figure out what the problem is.

It's Mark who speaks next. "Why… aren't you still with Rose?" he asks me.

"Hey, I was in there for a couple of hours." Is that their problem? They can't seriously think I didn't last that long, do they? "She got her fill, believe me."

"No, Tristan, it's not that," Reece says. "It's just… you didn't stay with her?"

"Stay with her?" I repeat, confusion washing over me. "What do you mean? I was in there plenty long enough to do what needed to be done. She liked it, too, believe me." I grin, and a low rumble of joy escapes my throat.

No one else thinks it's funny.

"Don't you think it would've been polite of you to spend the night with her? I mean… sleeping?" Eli asks. "This is only her second time, and she is probably scared.'

I scowl at him. "She's not scared. She had a good time. Why would I want to go to bed now? I'm on cloud… eleven!"

"Two steps above cloud nine?" Reece clarifies, and I nod. He shakes his head at me. "You're such a prick."

"Hey!" I interject. "I am not! You're just jealous that you haven't had a turn yet!"

"I'm not jealous, believe me." Reece continues to give me a disapproving look, but he's not worked up.

I try to settle back down. "Well, excuse me for wanting to share my success with the people I thought were supposed to be my friends!"

"Maybe we don't want to hear about you boning the girl we are all going to be with!" Mark spits. He does, in fact, look perturbed. He folds his arms across his chest.

I can't help but poke the bear. "Oh, don't worry, Marky," I say. "I'm sure she hasn't completely forgotten about you, now that she's had me. Not yet anyway."

I laugh, but Mark takes it personally and flies up off of the couch. "Stop being an asshole, Tristan!"

I spring to my feet, ready for a fight. It's been too damn long since

I had the chance to punch someone in the face. He won't be so pretty when I'm done with him.

"Hey, knock it off!" Eli says as he and Reece both get between us. "We need to be calm about this. It's not like any of us are happy about the situation, but it is what it is."

"That's right," Reece continues. "We can't beat each other up every time someone else sleeps with Rose, or we'll all be bruised and battered. So calm down."

I keep the grin on my face as Mark takes a step back and yanks at his hair in frustration. "We shouldn't be discussing what happens with Rose! This is supposed to be respectful... not a contest."

"But it is a contest," I remind him. "And I intend to win it."

"Well, if you're going to win and keep your so-called friends, you'd better figure out a way to do it without being such an asshat," Reece tells me.

I figure he's probably right. These guys are my friends, my allies, and I shouldn't be jeopardizing what's best for my pack just because I have a smart mouth. "Fine," I concede. "Goddess, I was just having some fun. You guys are lame."

I wave them off and head for the door, thinking they can go back to watching their movie again in peace. Obviously, they don't care to hear how things went with Rose and me the same way everyone wanted to know about Mark earlier this morning.

Maybe if he'd been keen to tell them, they would've realized they didn't want to know that either.

I walk out into the hallway and head for my room, but I hear hurried footsteps behind me and stop. Turning around, I see that it's Mark.

"What? You still wanna fight me?" I ask him.

He shakes his head. "No. I just... I wanted to talk to you in private," he mutters quietly.

"About what?" I fold my arms and lean back against the wall.

"About... Rose," he begins. "I know what you do in there is your business, but she–" He stops talking, his eyes widen, and I turn to see why.

It's Rose, walking down the hallway, wearing a dress–an actual dress, not the little pink nightie she had on before–and Shelby, Beta Adam's wife, is with her.

"Hi," Mark greets first.

Rose's face is a little pale, and I wonder if she's okay. "Hey," she greets back. I see that she's wearing my necklace, and I can't help but grin at her.

"Hi there, little flower," I say.

She smiles back at me, but Mark grimaces.

"What are you guys doing?" Shelby asks us. "Tristan, I figured you must not be feeling well with how quickly you took off out of Rose's room!" She sounds angry, and I see Rose elbow her.

My forehead furrows. "I, uh... I'm fine. Rose, did you want me to stay with you?" I've never spent the night with a woman before. I always leave or kick them out of my bed. I like to sleep alone. It hadn't even crossed my mind that she might expect me to act differently.

"No, I'm fine," she admits with a shrug. "Just thought it might be a nice night for a stroll in the garden. The moon is bright." Her smile doesn't reach her eyes, and when she looks at Mark, I see her eyes move back and forth slightly, like she isn't sure what to say to him.

"Rose, are you sure you're okay?" Mark asks, his tone soft and calm, but I can hear concern in every syllable.

This dude is starting to really fall for her.

I'm not sure how I feel about that, but I don't think I like it. She's my little flower.

"I'm fine." Her forced smile grows. "We just... did our job, and it's over. For now. So... everyone can go on about their day."

"Our job?" I ask her, feeling a little bit like a tool in more ways than one.

"Yeah, sure," she sighs with a shrug. "That's all this is, right? No need for tricky emotions to get involved. Just... do our job, fulfill the obligation, and get on with our lives, right?"

Does she really feel that way? If so, it makes me sad and confused. I realize I already have feelings for her, and I want her to like me, too.

Mark must agree with me. He starts to answer her. "Rose, that's not–"

"You know what?" Shelby says in her assertive tone, "I don't think either one of you has a right to tell Rose how to feel, especially after the way you've both treated her!"

"Shelby," Rose scolds, tugging on her arm. "Stop!" Her face is turning red, and I think it might be from embarrassment.

"They need to know!" Shelby exclaims. Looking at Mark, she says in an accusatory tone, "You, telling everyone how disappointed you were with her. She was a virgin! How was she supposed to know what to do?"

"Whaaat?" Mark nearly shrieks, and I am baffled, too. He definitely didn't say that.

Turning to look at me, Shelby says, "And you! Drilling into her like you were looking for oil only to get your fill and then abandon her, leaving her on the bed in pain from fucking her so damn hard! You animal!"

"Pain?" I repeat. "No, I didn't–" but I stop talking as I see tears in Rose's eyes.

"Come on, Rosey," Shelby cajoles, calling her by a nickname. "Let's go."

Rose is shaking her head as she walks away, leaving Mark and me flabbergasted.

"Did I hurt her?" I wonder.

"I'm sure you did, you sicko," he attacks, glaring at me. "We warned you."

"No, but… I tried to be gentle…."

"Why does she think I would say anything like that?" he questions. He turns to look at me again. "Did you… tell her I said that?"

"Me?" My eyes are wide. "No! I didn't mention you. Why would I?"

"To make her not like me anymore," he says with an accusatory tone. "So she'll like you more."

I guffaw. "No, I didn't say that, Mark. It wasn't me. Do you really think I'm the kind of guy who thinks I need to put other people down to make myself look better? I'm already the best."

He stares at me hard for a moment before he says, "That's a good point, except for you being the best part…. Well, who the hell was it, then?"

I think back to the conversation I had with Rose before we had sex, earlier today. "Oh, I know exactly who it was," I relay to Mark as the revelation hits me mid-sentence.

"Who?"

If I tell him, he'll go crazy and yell at her, which could make the king mad, so maybe I shouldn't.

"Emily," I blurt out, without regard to the consequences.

"That little bitch!" Mark yells, and he takes off down the hallway.

I don't know whether to laugh or cry about Mark, but I have more important matters to think about.

Does Rose hate me now?

CHAPTER 21: HAVING A BALL

Rose

The next day, Shelby wants to take me shopping. She says it will take my mind off of everything, but I'm not sure that's true.

After Tristan said, "Well, I guess I'll see you later," and leaped out of my bed, I'd lain there for several minutes, trying to figure out what to do. My body hurt, and I felt all alone.

I'd decided I needed to talk to Shelby, and after a tearful explanation as to what was bothering me, we'd gone for a little stroll.

And ran right into the two Alphas I was so embarrassed to see!

I had tried to play it off. I certainly didn't want them to know how upset they'd made me. But then Shelby had gone and let them both have it. I'd been so mortified, standing there, listening to her go on and on about how dreadful they both were.

We'd walked around the garden a bit, but then I'd come back to my room and tried to get some sleep.

Now, I am waiting for her to show up to take me to the village to shop. I don't have any money, and I don't need anything anyway, so I'm not even sure what we're doing, but I will go.

I have nothing better to do, after all.

"Are you ready?" Shelby asks, popping her head into the room.

I get up off the bed. "Yeah, I'm ready."

"Why the long face?" she asks as I walk over to her. "Those stupid boys are both set straight now. You don't need to worry about them anymore."

"I'm not sure I'll be the best company for you," I tell her. "I've been trying to get my mind off them, but I just can't."

"You need a dress for the ball tonight," Shelby says as she pulls me out the door. "You have two other perfectly good Alphas waiting for you who aren't acting like jackasses."

She has a point, but what are the chances Reece and Eli will feel differently about me than Mark and Tristan?

We get a few steps down the hallway before she stops and knocks on a door near the Alphas' rooms, and my heart leaps into my chest. "What are you doing?" I ask her.

"Relax!" she tells me. "I'm getting Kelly."

My heart falls back into place when Kelly comes out into the hallway and greets us with a happy smile.

We take off for the village on foot, and by the time we get there, after listening to the other girls talk about how much fun the ball will be, I'm in a better mood. Maybe it'll be fun, after all.

I still don't know how I'm supposed to pay for this. I have no money, and if I've earned anything yet, it has gone straight to my parents.

We walk into a boutique, and Shelby goes straight to the back where they keep the gowns. She pulls up a bright purple gown. "This one is so pretty!" she exclaims. "It would look so great on you, Kelly."

"Yeah, I like it," Kelly admits. "The blue is pretty, too!"

They spend several minutes looking at different dresses before they notice I am just standing there.

"Rose, aren't you going to find a dress?" Kelly asks me.

"Oh, uh… I don't know," I stammer. I feel my cheeks turning red. "I mean… they seem to be kind of expensive."

"So?" Shelby asks with a snort. "Honey, you know you're not paying for it, right?"

I only stare at her, not sure what to say.

"The king has a tab," Kelly explains. "Any guests of his in the castle will have their ball gowns paid for. No worries."

"That includes you, silly!" Shelby tells me, but rather than laughing at me, they go back to looking at the dresses.

I see an emerald green dress that catches my eye, so I go over to look at it, but as I pull on it, I feel it tugged in the opposite direction.

"Hey! That's my dress!" I hear a familiar voice shout at me from the other side of the rack.

My breath catches in my throat. I can't see her because the rack is too tall, but I know who it is before she stretches up on her tiptoes.

"Well, well, well, if it isn't the fucking breeder," Emily snarls. "Funny I should meet you here. Are you even going to bother to come to the ball? I don't see the point. It's not like anyone will dance with you because they want to. Though the poor Alphas might feel obligated to."

I let go of the dress, starting to walk away from her. I have nothing to say.

She's probably right, anyway. No one will want to dance with me, and if they do, they'll be disappointed, just like the two men I've slept with.

She doesn't let me walk away, though. She comes around the rack, two of her friends in tow. "By the way," she begins as Shelby and Kelly step toward me, alarmed looks on their faces. "I'm super pissed that you talked to Mark about me!"

I turn and look at her. "I didn't–"

"Save it!" she shouts. "He came to my room last night to talk to me about it, to tell me that he found out that you had heard how disappointed he was. He obviously didn't want me to talk about that. Why the hell would you mention it to him, bitch?"

"I didn't!" I say, turning to glare at her.

"I told him," Shelby spits out, stepping over. "It was me, Emily. Leave her alone."

Emily's eyes narrow on Shelby. "You might think you're pretty fucking special because your husband is the Beta, but my cousin is the king! Don't you forget that!" She shoves Shelby hard in the shoulder.

"Hey!" I shout stepping over to her. "Don't do that!"

Emily turns and looks at me for a minute before she starts laughing. "Or what? I bet you don't even have a wolf yet, breeder! What are you going to do?"

I have no response for her. I don't want to fight her in the middle of the boutique, so I just stare her down until she turns to her friends.

"Come on, let's go somewhere else. I guess I didn't realize this store let in beggars and rejects!" She walks past me and hits me hard with her shoulder. My hands clench but then unclench, and I want to punch her in the face. But I stop myself. I know how angry my parents will be if I find a way to ruin this for them.

When they are gone, I find myself shaking. My blood is boiling, and I feel sweat breaking out around my chest.

"I'm sorry, Rose," Shelby sympathizes, coming over to wrap her arms around me. "I didn't know she'd be here."

I say nothing but rest my forehead on her shoulder. I just don't understand why Emily has to be so mean! She's the one who will get to spend the rest of her life with the next Alpha King—not me. She should be happy about that.

But she seems so jealous of my position, that i get to sleep with four Alphas, she can hardly control herself.

"The green would look really pretty on you," Kelly says, trying to stabilize the situation.

"I don't want a dress Emily touched," I spit out.

"What about the burgundy one?" she asks me.

Shelby and I part, and I dab at my tears. I still have to find a dress. I still have to go to the ball, even if no one will want to dance with me.

The burgundy one will do just as well as any others, so I take it from the rack and head to the dressing room to try it on. I barely make it into the room before the tears start falling.

I try to stay quiet because I don't want to alert my new friends, but I can't help but sob. What am I doing here? What in the world made me think I could actually do this job?

Then I remember—I never did think I could do it. I'm not here because I want to be. I'm here because I have no choice. My parents insisted I come. Now I'm here, and I'm failing miserably.

Exactly as my parents said I would.

If I can only find a way to make the Alphas really like me, maybe when this is all over, my parents won't hear about what a failure I am, but so far… all I've done is embarrass myself.

"Rose, are you all right?" Shelby calls, and I can hear concern in her voice.

"I'm fine," I lie, wiping at my tears. I have to stop crying or she'll come in, and I really don't want to change clothes in front of her, not that she hasn't already seen everything I have to offer.

Somehow, I manage to get myself under control and change into the ballgown. When I step out, they are both waiting.

Kelly and Shelby gasp and cover their mouths. My first instinct is that I must look ridiculous.

But then Shelby cheers, "I've never seen anything more beautiful in my life!"

"You look gorgeous!" Kelly agrees.

"When Emily sees you… she's going to be so jealous!" Shelby continues.

"And my brother is going to lose his shit!" Kelly adds.

I feel like they're just being nice, but when I turn to look at myself in the mirror, I do think the dress looks beautiful on me.

Maybe I am a huge disappointment to everyone, and maybe I'll fall on my face tonight, too.

But at least I'll look good doing it.

CHAPTER 22: IT IS A CONTEST, AFTER ALL

I PACE around my room and continue to curse loudly at the walls. I think back to when I went to confront Emily about the lies she had spun about me to Rose.

It's impossible not to recognize the way Emily looks at me—like I'm a slab of juicy meat she can't wait to sink her teeth into. She stares straight at me as we talk, telling me she knows I secretly loathe being with Rose.

I won't lie; overall, it has been a very uncomfortable experience... not because I don't want to be with Rose but because I hate sharing her with anyone.

The way Emily is looking at me as we stand at her door is weird. She expects me to break down and tell her what she wants to hear. I've been used to female attention all my life, but this unsettling crawling sensation up my spine is very new. I have never despised a woman this much.

And I know exactly why.

I am consumed by Rose.

I don't want her to think about me and someone else together in any form. I don't want her to think I am only with her out of duty or would blatantly go around telling people how I hate spending time with her. Fuck, I want to spend every waking moment with her.

If she sometimes entertains the thought of me being the person for her when this is all over, I don't want her to be jealous now because a strange woman thinks I'm available, and she goes around making fake allegations.

I'm not available, not even for the king's cousin. I want to belong to Rose. I actually believe I already belong to her–I was the one to take her virginity–and I wish she knew that.

I am praying for a chance to talk to her and put her worries to rest. Seeing her cry really messed me up mentally. I never want to be the source of her pain, physical or emotional. I hope I get a chance to tell her at the ball tonight.

This brings me to the mission I need to complete before the ball: confronting Tristan. Anything or anyone who dares to make Rose sad will have to pay the price, and I'll be enforcing that penalty.

One would think that after all the warnings we all gave him about being gentle with her, he would have at least tried. But he had gone ahead and hurt her. Then the idiot had slid off her to rush out of the room and left her confused and in pain.

I had to talk to Tristan, maybe even punch him in his pompous face, both for hurting her and even daring to touch what's mine.

It's ridiculous to think of Rose as solely mine; I knew the deal when I agreed to this madness. But it was going to be a difficult ride given that I really have fallen head first like an idiot for Rose.

I hesitate at the door to Tristan's room. I know I should knock politely, but I am not thinking straight and don't think the fool deserves an ounce of respect. I ball my fist and pound on the wooden door once, twice, and then barge in without waiting for an answer.

Tristan looks up from behind a desk. I can see him raise an eyebrow. I am not here to exchange pleasantries or sex tips, so I walk purposefully toward him.

Tristan pushes the papers he has in front of him to the side before leaning back in his chair and regarding me coldly… the arrogant, self-centered bastard.

"How dare you hurt Rose! You know she is innocent and fragile. When will you grow up and understand that she is not one of the cheap whores you are used to?" I spit immediately.

He makes no move to stand up and his face remains unreadable.

"I had no intentions of hurting Rose," he says simply and offers no explanation. I feel myself getting worked up, and I want him to match my mood at the moment; his stoic reactions are doing nothing to calm my frustrations at him and this whole arrangement. I'd appreciate a bit more passion from him. Rose was hurt by him, and his coolness is sickening.

"Well, you did. You have no regard for anyone's feelings but your own, Tristan, and that is a problem. You can do that out there, but not to Rose, or else–" I don't get to finish my statement because he jumps to his feet and leans his hands on his hips, using the desk in front of him for balance.

"Who died and made you the behavioral expert? Do you think you have the right to go around telling people how to treat Rose? She is not yours, Mark, just because you won the right to claim her virginity. It's clouding your perceptions about the situation," Tristan says coolly.

Then he continues, "Rose might choose to be with me and not the guy who supposedly didn't enjoy his time with her. At least I didn't go and tell the whole world embarrassing facts about my night with her."

I feel bile rising in my chest like a volcano. He knew that whatever had been said wasn't true.

"I didn't have any embarrassing moments regarding my night with Rose. Actually, I don't recall giving any details at all. You know as much as I do that Emily made up that lie for her own amusement," I say as I regard him coldly. I am measuring the distance between us in my head, wondering if my arm could reach across the width of his desk to give him a solid knockout punch.

"It's funny, then, how you can justify what happened. Also, may I remind you that you hurt Rose, and I had to comfort her. Yet, you come in here to condemn me for something I did with no intention of hurting her. You are not the only one who cares for Rose, you know," he continues as his features darken.

I try to steady my breathing and swallow down the burning rage in me. I know this is stupid, but I can't help feeling anger. I'm angry at the king for putting this situation on us. I'm angry at Tristan for causing pain to Rose, however unintentional he claims it was. I'm angry at Emily for cooking up a disgusting lie, and angry at all the Alphas standing in line to bed Rose.

I even feel angry at Rose, even though I know she doesn't deserve it, for buying into the lies. I feel guilty for even having that emotion, to feel upset at her.

And lastly, I feel angry at myself for not reassuring her about my feelings; angry at myself for falling for her so fast and so hard.

A low groan escapes my throat.

I need something or someone to take out my frustrations on. I pray Tristan says something about Rose that gives me an excuse to punch him.

"For the record, my night with Rose was magical. I told Emily as much, and if I have to tell the rest of the world, I will," I declare firmly and feel a wave of relief sweeping over me at the thought of bringing the truth forward.

"Then why were you so tight-lipped about it earlier? People are bound to speculate. You should have clarified right away," he suggests. His reasoning is sound, but who cares what other people think?

"I don't talk about my private affairs. I don't kiss and tell. People are already well aware of the situation we all are in, and I have no need to tell anyone about my night with Rose. What Rose and I do is between the two of us. I respect her as much as I do myself. I was probably wrong in not telling her my true feelings to calm her doubts."

I wasn't finished. "But you, on the other hand, used her and discarded her like a dirty tissue. Do you have no ounce of compassion in that huge body of yours?"

Tristan looks at me and stands up straight. He crosses his arms across his chest in a contemplative stance. The rise and fall of his chest makes it clear that he's fighting to maintain his composure.

"I will have to learn to do better," Tristan states firmly. "I have never spent a whole night with a woman before," he confesses. "Rose isn't like any woman I've been with before. I was wrong and selfish," he exhales. "I will learn. I hope she will give me another chance and teach me how she wants me to love her."

The last part he says in such a hushed tone that I have to strain just to hear him. It seems like it is a personal thought that isn't meant for my ears.

"I think this arguing back and forth is doing no good to anyone. If Rose senses this dissonance between us, it will only make her uncomfortable, and knowing her, she will probably blame herself for the bickering. I think we ought to all take a step back and not act like horny teenagers competing for affection," I suggest.

Surprisingly, Tristan nods in agreement. "Let's give her the chance to actually follow her own instincts and feelings. In the process, let's just treat her as the precious gem that she is."

I think I hear Tristan mutter under his breath something like 'little flower,' but I can't be certain. I guess we all have a different name for Rose. Clearly, we are all in too deep. We have to pull back, and I hope the other Alphas will because I feel in my heart I won't be able to even if I try.

I shake my head of those thoughts and continue. "She is far from her home and had never been with a man before us. She doesn't deserve all this nonsense. She deserves to be protected, loved, and cared for," I say with a wistful tone, and Tristan continues nodding.

'Loved by me, I hope,' I think silently as I turn to leave. I have to prepare for the ball, and I hope I will get a chance to talk to Rose, my sweet baby love.

CHAPTER 23: LEAVING... WITH THE GIRL

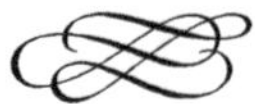

I hold the stray hand that's crawling down my bicep and turn. "Do you just go around touching men, Emily?"

It's a firm warning I'm giving off since I'm not trying to play coy about what is happening here. And neither is she, apparently. She leans away, her eyes bearing the singed pride of someone who has never been rejected before. "Only those I wouldn't mind giving a good time," she replies.

I know now that there is a Moon Goddess–and that she makes her payments with karma.

Maybe I was an asshole in my previous life, or else she'd have compassion on me and make Rose the one that's telling me this, not this woman I've known for only a few days.... Well, I've also only known Rose for just a couple of days, but that's different; I actually want to get to know Rose.

"While that is an interesting offer. I'm not interested," I say firmly, not trying to sound like a complete asshole... yet.

"Is it because you are afraid you won't be the winner of the competition and get to take my hand as your wife? You don't have to be scared about that. It's just a dance. I've seen how you've been looking at me the past few days. I won't bite. We could have a splendid night together."

I am trying not to raise my voice as she continues to eye me and blink her lashes. The action reminds me of a bird preparing to take flight. I pray someone, or something, saves me from this woman. I want to be with Rose but find myself wondering what will happen if I have to be the one to call this woman my Luna. I shake my head forcefully; I don't even want to think of that possibility.

Where is Rose?

I look around the room but see no sign of her. I glance over at the podium and see the king speaking with Mark and Tristan; I can't hear what is being discussed thanks to the loud music and distance. The exchange looks serious, and I wish I was better at lip reading.

A tap on my shoulder brings my attention back to my present position. I pray it is not yet another woman here to ask me for a dance. Was it the new era that changed the roles we were all accustomed to of the man being the one to ask a woman for a dance, and not the other way around?

I turn around, but the words of disapproval at the tip of my tongue die when I see Eli. Certainly, he's not a woman, and he's not here to ask me to dance.

He looks fresh in a starched shirt and bow tie. I lift my hand to my neck and try to loosen my tie. Eli looks comfortable in his formal attire, but I feel like my tie is slowly getting tighter and trying to choke me. I find myself missing my casual clothes.

"Want to dance?" I ask, only joking.

Eli takes a step back, "Huh?" He looks confused.

"Joking," I mutter before continuing. "Hey." I nervously look around and exhale with relief to find that Emily seems to have given up on her agenda and moved to another man I don't recognize.

"Why are your eyes darting around like you're tracking prey?" Eli asks as he also follows the direction of my gaze. I chuckle at his assessment.

"More like I am the prey. I thought you were Emily or someone similar," I say and take a glass of champagne from a tray when a servant passes by. Eli does the same and returns his attention to me.

"Did you forget she might be your future Luna?" he cajoles and elbows me playfully.

"Or yours," I return and smirk at him.

"I am glad Tristan and Mark have called a truce. The king also spoke to them about their fight; it was just creating unnecessary tension," Eli sighs seemingly relieved and then takes a sip of his drink.

I take a sip from my glass. So that is what they were talking about when I spotted them with the king earlier.

"Aren't you jealous about the prospect of sharing Rose?" I ask him.

Eli inclines his head to the side and seems to smile. "No. I know once I get my turn with her, the rest of you are history," he says with a playful smirk.

I want to respond to his cocky reply, but I bite my tongue. There is no need to start our own fight right here and now. I also know he's just saying that in an attempt at a light-hearted joke, but I fail to find the humor in it.

"I see," I nod and take a huge gulp of my drink. I really need the alcoholic liquid courage right now.

The fast-paced music that is playing stops after a minute, and a soft tune begins. I listen to it, and I imagine myself slow dancing to it with Rose. I note that Eli's eyes are now focusing on the entrance to the ballroom. I take note of how his eyes seem to sparkle and widen at whatever he is seeing.

Everyone else seems to be looking in that direction too. I turn to see what has grabbed everyone's attention and almost choke on pure air when I finally set my eyes on the angel making her way into the room.

The sound of the music seems to fade as I watch her seemingly float into the room. Everyone else disappears, and all I see is her.

She is dressed in a burgundy gown that shows off her delicately molded figure. Her waist is slim and her skin lustrous; I swear she seems to be glowing under the dim lighting of the room. Her hair is gathered in an intricate design on top of her head. The little decorations in it sparkle as she walks. Her head is bowed, and I wonder if she even realizes how she demands attention without even trying. She is perfect.

When she raises her head, she shows off pearly white teeth at the couple she walked in with. I find myself strolling toward her as if she had silently called to me. Before I know it, I am standing in front of her.

She regards me before doing a subtle curtsey and smiles. A little dimple forms on her left cheek, and I feel like my blood is flowing in the wrong direction within my body.

A crash somewhere in the room reminds me that there are other people around. I turn around to find the source of the noise and see Emily walk away from shards of glass that are on the floor. A servant rushes to the site to clean the mess. I turn and refocus my attention on the belle of this ball.

I stretch my arm to her. "May I have this dance?" I ask, ignoring Emily's commotion as I fight back the butterflies that have built a small army in my stomach. I have never felt this nervous about asking a woman for a dance before, but this is no ordinary woman. I haven't even had much time with her, yet I already understand why Mark and Tristan have been squabbling over her.

I pray she doesn't say no and leave me here to wallow in my embarrassment. After the way she was when she had come to confront Mark and Tristan... well when Shelby confronted them on her behalf... she might not want to indulge me, thinking we're all jerks. Cut from different cloths, but jerks all the same. I'd heard the commotion through the bedroom door.

I almost want to jump and touch the ceiling when she actually nods and places a gloved palm on my arm. It's nothing major, just a dance, but to me, it feels like winning the first battle.

I lead her to the dance floor. It seems the Moon Goddess is looking out for me now, as at that exact moment a sweet love song begins to play.

I draw her close and inhale her scent. She smells like a fruity garden, and it's dizzying in a way that makes me want to sweep her into my arms and carry her somewhere where it can just be the two of us.

"Are you okay?" I whisper into her ear as we sway to the rhythm. I can hear her gulp.

"Yeah," she sighs but I don't believe her.

"You look beautiful. And on behalf of all the Alphas, I am sorry for everything. I promise we are not all jerks."

I relax when she chuckles.

"I didn't know the king had a dress tailor-made for you," I say, and this time she laughs out loud. The sound warms my heart.

"It wasn't tailor-made for me. I found it at some shop this afternoon," she admits.

"Huh. You could have fooled me. I would have sworn it was made with you in mind," I reassure her.

She leans back and regards me. I know she is trying to catch the lie in my facial expression.

"You flatter me, Alpha Reece."

I draw her even closer to me. The feel of her warm, slim body against mine is making my heart beat increase, and I can feel a tent beginning to build in my pants. "I don't aim to flatter, as I speak nothing but the truth, my angel."

She smiles and looks around nervously. I wonder what is going on inside her head. I see her gaze rest on a particular location in the room for a length of time and her smile vanishes. I swirl her around so as to see who, or what, she is looking at. I see Tristan watching us with a scowl on his face.

"If you feel uncomfortable, maybe we can leave this place," I suggest.

"Wouldn't that be considered rude… since I just got here, and the ball is far from being over?" She innocently licks her lips, and I feel like my knees will give out supporting the weight of my body. I gaze into her eyes and move my face toward hers. I am tempted to kiss her, but I don't want to steal the kiss. I want her to give it to me when the time comes out of her own free will.

"Tonight is my night with you. We can go, and if you feel like you are not up for going that far tonight, we could just lay in bed, and I will hold you throughout the night. After all you have been through, I won't push you to do anything that you don't want to do," I try to reassure her.

She blinks at me. I have a distinct feeling she doesn't believe me. I would love to make passionate love to her and erase the pain and her past experiences, but if she says no, I would be okay just holding her all through the night.

"You are expected to make love to me though," she states plainly. "That's why I'm here." Her words feel like a sword to my heart. She really sees this whole thing as nothing but a duty. I want to show her that it can be way more beautiful than she thinks.

"My angel, with me, you are not just an object for breeding. You are a gorgeous woman who deserves to feel pleasure. Come with me tonight. I promise to give you all of the control. I want to teach you how to not only receive pleasure but to give it freely."

I look into her eyes and plead with my own. She bites her lips.... This woman will be the death of me. She nods. I take her hand and lead her out of the ballroom.

Tonight will be romantic. Tonight will be beautiful and magical, just like she is.

CHAPTER 24: THE NEXT ALPHA

Rose

THIS ISN'T how I thought the ball was going to go earlier in the day when I was picking out this gown. I expected to stay for a few hours, to possibly dance with all of the Alphas, but when Reece gave me the opportunity to leave, I took it.

After all, I saw Emily there, and if I stayed, I might've had to speak to her again.

Or be further tormented.

This is a much better idea.

He holds my hand tightly as we walk down the hallway. We aren't hurrying, but at the same time, he isn't slowing down, and I have to rush a little to keep up with him. His legs are a lot longer than mine, after all.

We reach a room near where I saw Tristan and Mark speaking the night before, and I have to imagine this is Reece's room. Of the four, I imagine he is probably the neatest, the tidiest, and I guess his room is probably kept immaculately.

So when he opens the door and has to push some dirty clothes aside with his foot, I'm surprised.

"Sorry," he says. "I was expecting the maids to be in here while we were at the ball."

I glance around and see some empty beer bottles, a discarded plate of food, and some more dirty clothes strewn about. It almost makes me laugh.

Not quite the beautiful flowers or candlelight I've been used to.

But the bed is made, and it looks soft and inviting, the light blue comforter pulled back on one corner. The bed beckons to us, even if the room doesn't.

Reece stands next to me, a questioning expression on his face. "Are you sure… you wanna do this?"

I look at him, my eyebrows raised. I remember what he said to me earlier about me being able to back out if I want to, that we could just lie there, and he would hold me.

It was a sweet gesture, it really was. After I'd gotten so mixed up with my emotions about Mark, who apparently wasn't impressed with me at all, and Tristan, who was a wham-bam-thank-you-ma'am kinda guy, I thought just lying in Reece's arms and chatting would be a nice change of pace.

But it wouldn't be fair. He shouldn't be punished because he was nice. This is his chance to become king. Who am I to take it away from him?

Unless, of course, he is just trying to get out of having sex with me.

That makes perfect sense, now that I think about it, based on everything he's heard about me from the men who've come before him.

"Do you… do you want to?" I ask him, my voice quivering a little.

"Do I want to… make love to you?" he asks, and I realize he's used a more intimate term than what I had been calling it in my head.

I nod. I don't see the point in correcting him.

A smile pulls up the corners of his mouth. "Well, yeah, of course, I do," he says. "Why wouldn't I?"

I can think of a lot of reasons, but I don't see the point in listing them off for him.

He reaches over and cups my cheek with his hand. "I just want to make sure you're ready, Rose. I want to give you an opportunity to really explore what your body is capable of. I want to bring you pleasure like you've never imagined."

I feel my face catch fire, and my core begins to tighten. This handsome Alpha is so concerned about me that he cares about how I feel?

He steps closer to me, and his lips graze my mouth lightly. I imagine this is what an angel's wings must feel like.

I respond to him, pressing into him as his arms encircle me, and I run my fingers through his hair. The kiss deepens, and I taste him for the first time. He tastes like punch, a bit of strawberry and orange, and I imagine he must've had a drink of something fruity at the ball.

I didn't get a chance for anything like that.

But I'm okay with it.

Reece leads me over to the bed without releasing my lips. He kicks his shoes off and drops his mouth to my neck, softly peppering my burning flesh with his cool kisses. "I want to undress you," he says quietly. "Will you let me?"

"Y-yes," I whisper.

He takes his time, carefully removing my jewelry first before he bends down and unbuckles my shoes. When he stands back up, he is breathless, but not from exertion. His eyes are twinkling as he quietly says, "May I unzip your gown?"

I can't breathe either, so I simply turn around. His fingers brush my shoulders, and then he lowers his hands and takes the zipper between his fingers, slowly tugging it down. The lower it goes, the more my flesh tingles with anticipation.

The dress drops to the ground, and I turn around. I am standing in front of him in my underwear, a matching lacy green silk panties and bra set, and he is fully dressed.

He is smiling widely at me, though.

I find my voice and say, "I think you're overdressed."

Reece chuckles and says, "Can you help me with that?"

I feel my face heat up again, but I don't mind helping him. He doffs his jacket while I work on his tie and toss that aside, my trembling fingers moving to his buttons as he pulls out his belt.

Somehow, he even manages to get out of his socks without stopping, and I get to the bottom button, my eyes caressing every rippling muscle, my fingertips longing to drag over them.

When I reach the bottom of his shirt, he says, "Keep going," and gives me a playful smile, shrugging out of it. I grin back at him and unbutton his pants, tugging carefully on the zipper, and he slides them down off of his hips. He's wearing red briefs, and he looks incredible.

"We're even now," he tells me.

I nod and bite my bottom lip.

"Would you like to lay down?" he asks me.

Still unable to draw a deep breath, I move to the bed, and he comes with me, catching my lips with his as we both recline on the pillows. His kisses are still soft and loving, and as his hands roam over me, he takes his time, caressing me gently.

In a way, it reminds me of Mark, but I can't let myself think of him right now. I need to focus on Reece.

He leans back and looks at me. "What would you like for me to do, Rose?"

I stare back at him, blankly. "Wh-what?" I ask him.

Grinning at me, he says, "Where do you want me to touch you?"

Shaking my head slightly, I admit, "I don't know."

"Take control, Rose. You're in charge."

I don't know what to say or do. I don't even know what to think. But he's just lying there on the pillow, gazing at me.

So… I move to him, leaning over him and pressing my lips to his. He responds, kissing me back, and I run my hands along his chest, letting my nails drag over his abdomen. I stop short of the bulge in his underwear, but he whispers, "Rose? I'm yours, remember?"

And I realize he's serious. He wants me to do whatever I'd like.

My hand drops lower, and I am touching his rock-hard dick

through his underwear. He groans into my mouth, and I think he likes that, so I grab him harder, running my hand along his shaft.

If he was naked, this would be easier. I decide he needs to be.

Grabbing hold of his waistband, I yank his underwear down. He helps me by lifting his hips, and I pull them down. His cock springs out of them, and I am amazed at how big he is, too.

It must just be part of being an Alpha....

Now that he is naked, I want to touch him everywhere. I have read about women taking a man's shaft into their mouth, but I don't think I'm ready for that. I will stick to my hands for now.

The sounds he is making let me know that he really likes this.

I feel myself growing wetter and wetter as my muscles tighten just thinking about him.

His hand grazes my breast through my bra, and it feels good, but I want it to feel better. I reach around and unhook my bra. It falls to my elbows, and he gasps, smiling at me.

I take it off and toss it away, and he begins to rub my breasts, fingering my nipples. I close my eyes and enjoy it, but as good as it feels, I'm still not satisfied.

I lean over him, and he takes a nipple between his lips, massaging the other with his hand, and I find my heart beginning to race.

I find myself rocking back and forth on his cock, but my panties are in the way. I need them off. I don't want to pull away from his expert mouth, though.

Reaching back, I try to slide them off, and Reece realizes I'm struggling and helps me. When they are discarded, and we are both completely nude, I straddle him, rubbing myself along his shaft. I am so wet, and he is so hard, it feels so good without him even penetrating me.

But he has to do that in order to have his chance at getting me pregnant.

I'm just not sure how that will work with me on top of him.

Pulling back slightly, I look down at him, biting my bottom lip.

"What is it, darlin'?" he asks me, and I like how sweet that name sounds. Not darling–not something so formal–darlin', like we have known each other for years.

"Can you… help me?" I ask, feeling my face flame again.

"Sure. With what?"

I don't know how to explain. I was sort of hoping he'd just… figure it out. I look down at his massive cock, and he gets the picture.

"Yeah, yeah, sure, darlin'," he says. "Push up onto your knees." He grabs hold of his dick and holds it upright, and then he guides me over the top of him so that he is poised at my entrance. As I lower down, Reece uses his hand to hold me open so I can slide around him.

"Gooooddesss," I moan as I come down, consuming him. He chuckles slightly, and once I am on him, he pulls his hand back and places both of them on my hips.

I begin to work up and down, and he uses his hands to guide me. It feels so good, I feel myself beginning to come undone already.

"Do whatever feels good to you, Rose," he says, his tone still soft and gentle.

I'm not sure what might feel better, but what I am doing already feels great, so I keep doing it until I feel my muscles begin to spasm around him.

Reece continues to touch me, rubbing my breasts and my bottom, but then he slides his thumb back inside of my folds and finds my most sensitive area. He strokes it, pressing hard, pinching, and with each touch, I feel myself slip further and further over the edge.

I fall over the ledge then, panting and moaning. I continue to move my hips the best I can, but it's hard when I feel like my entire body is tightened around his hard cock.

After a few moments, Reece starts to buck beneath me, increasing the pace until we are both breathless and crying out, and then, I feel his seed filling me.

Immediately, I climb off him, lying down on my back. I don't want a single one of his chances to go to waste.

"Rose, are you okay?" he asks, still breathless but obviously concerned.

I nod my head, still unable to speak, but when I can finally talk again, all I can manage to say is, "Swimmers."

Reece bursts out laughing and then drops down and kisses me. "You're amazing, you know that?" he asks.

I'm not sure what I've said that has made him react that way, but I smile back at him.

"Thank you, Rose," he says. "That was incredible. Would you like to stay here with me tonight? Or if you're more comfortable, we can move to your room, and I can stay with you there."

I am so tired, I can't imagine putting that gown back on now. "Stay," I tell him, resting a hand on his arm.

His response… "Always."

CHAPTER 25: SLIGHTLY EMBARRASSING

Reece

It had taken me forever to fall asleep the night before, but not because I wasn't comfortable or happy, which was often the case when I couldn't sleep. No, this time, it was the exact opposite. I simply didn't want to take my eyes off Rose. I've slept with a lot of women in my life, but none as beautiful as her, none as graceful, intelligent, and kind.

In the morning, her bright eyes had locked onto mine, and all I could do was grin at her. I'd helped her get her gown back on and gotten dressed myself before offering to walk her back to her room.

I can tell Rose is a little flustered. "Do you think... anyone will see us?" she asks.

"I'm not sure," I reply as we approach the bedroom door. "Will it bother you if someone does?"

She shrugs. "I don't know. It's just... I'm wearing my gown. I'm pretty sure that makes this what some people call a walk of shame. Not that I'm ashamed of you or anything."

I chuckle at her. "Well, I can see why that might be a concern under some circumstances, but in this case, darlin', everyone already knows that you and I had sex last night. So... I wouldn't worry about it."

I'd meant to make her feel better, but her face is turning that pink color it changes to when she is embarrassed.

I lean down and press my lips to her temple. "Rose, if you're embarrassed of me, that's one thing, but I am certainly not embarrassed of you. I can't wait for everyone in the world to know we made love. As a matter of fact, I'd go scream it from the top of the castle if I had the choice."

She looks a little mortified. "I won't do that," I assure her. "My point is, I had an amazing time with you. That was the best sex I've ever had in my life, and I am proud to be walking out of this room with you right now."

"Really?" she asks, her nose crinkling slightly as she questions my explanation.

"Yes! Absolutely!"

She blushes again, but this isn't the same kind of embarrassment. I put my hand on the small of her back and guide her to the door. "Do you want me to stick my head out first?"

"No," she says. "I'm not embarrassed by you, Reece. I just... didn't know for sure how you felt."

I pull her against my chest and stroke her cheek with my palm. "I feel like... you're my sweet little darlin', and I want to be with you every moment of every day."

She melts against me, and I hold her tight. It's hard to know that I'm going to have to hand her over to Eli soon. I hope this isn't the last time I get to be with her. To think this could all be over soon, that she could be pregnant, and none of this will be necessary, makes my heart heavy.

As much as I would like to be king, I don't want to marry Emily. Maybe, if I don't win, I can keep Rose... forever. At the moment, I think that would make me the real winner.

When I can tell she's all right, I open the bedroom door, and keeping her hand in mine, I step out. There's no one in the hallway, and her room isn't far away.

We only make it a few steps before the door next to mine creaks open, and Mark steps out, looking a little ragged, like maybe he didn't sleep too well the night before.

"Oh, hi," he says, and I can tell this is just bad timing. He isn't trying to run into us. "Rose, good morning," he says, smiling at her.

She swallows hard. "Hi, Mark," she says, and I can tell she is upset at him. I know what Emily has told her. I also know it isn't true. I should've mentioned it to her the night before when she was lying in my arms, and we were chatting about life, but Mark was the furthest thing from my mind, and I saw no reason to remind her of him.

He drops his eyes, and I can tell he's in pain. She's not happy either, so I pull her away, leading her to her room. He walks down the hallway in the other direction.

At her door, I say, "Rose, you need to talk to him. Emily… is a liar. He never said anything bad about you."

She arches an eyebrow. "Are you sure about that?"

"Yes, I am," I tell her. "It might be in my best interest to tell you otherwise, but… I don't want anything to upset you, especially not Emily's lies."

She takes a deep breath and then says, "Thank you, Reece."

I smile at her. "Of course. Now, you have a great day, and hopefully, I will see you soon." I lean down and press my lips to hers, and she kisses me back.

Opening the door for her, I watch her go into her room, and when she closes the door behind her, I feel like I've lost a bit of my soul.

I head back to my room to shower and make myself presentable for breakfast with the other Alphas. I'm tired, but I'll survive. I've been tired before. When I come out of the bathroom, my Beta, Wessley, is there, leaning against the table where I do most of my work, looking at me with his eyebrows raised.

He is a bit older than me. He was my father's Beta before me, so he's almost old enough to be my dad. Still, we get along fairly well.

That doesn't mean I want to talk about sex with him, though.

He's not concerned about whether or not I had a good time, anyway. He just wants to know one thing.

"Well? Did you take advantage of your try?"

If everyone is as concerned about my sperm as Wessley, it will have its own spot on the nightly news.

"I did, Wessley," I assure him, finishing getting ready to go.

"And?"

"And what?" I ask him. "Does she look pregnant? Smell pregnant? Sound pregnant?"

He rolls his eyes at me. "I'm just wondering if you think you got a good one in her, that's all."

I scoff at him. "Yes, I do. I sent in my best men. All of 'em." I shake my head and walk out the door. I need to go or I'll be late. "Don't worry about it, Wessley. I gave it my all. My old man would be proud."

He chuckles under his breath and leaves to go take care of some business while I'm socializing.

When I walk into the breakfast room, the other three Alphas are already there. Tristan is in the middle of one of his loud, outlandish stories, but he cuts it short as I take my seat.

"Well?" Mark asks.

"Well… what?" I say, spreading my napkin over my lap.

"Did she… is she… okay?"

I look at him for a moment. "I thought you were the one who said you didn't want to talk about how we all did with her."

"I don't," he clarifies. "I just want to make sure she's okay. Some people didn't manage to make her so happy afterward." He glares at Tristan.

"Hey, I'm learning! We talked about this. I thought we were okay now." Tristan narrows his eyes back at Mark.

"Let's not fight!" Eli interjects. "Come on, guys. We need to try to get along. For Rose's sake."

I want to tell Eli that he doesn't even know her, but I don't think that's helpful. Besides, Eli has a point.

We eat in near silence, and it's clear that none of us are particularly happy with one another. I want to be the only one that gets to be with Rose, but I understand that she has feelings for all of these men, not just me. I can't be selfish.

"Hey, do you guys wanna go play basketball after this?" I ask as we finish breakfast. "Just hang out like friends and stop being angry at one another for a little while?"

"I'm not angry at anyone," Eli says with a shrug.

"Sure, I'll play," Tristan says, his tone conveying he might just want a chance to lord over us with his height and girth.

"I'm kind of busy," Mark mutters.

"Come on," Eli probes. "We can't play without you. We need even teams."

Mark grumbles a bit, but ultimately, he says, "Fine. I'll play."

I feel a bit lighter as we all stand up and head to our rooms to change clothes before we go outside. I was hoping I'd see Rose, but I don't, even though I linger in the hallway for a while. I feel disappointed, but I have to go on like it doesn't bother me, like I'm not missing her already.

I enter my room to grab some shorts and a T-shirt, but I choose to linger by the bed for a moment. It's been made, and I would guess that the sheets have even been changed, but that doesn't change the fact that I can remember how good it felt to be with her last night.

And if I breathe deeply enough... I can still smell her.

CHAPTER 26: ELI'S ROD

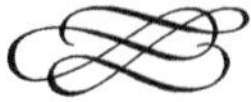

I don't have much planned for the day. In fact, after a long soak in the tub, I intend to just sit around and read until Eli lets me know what his plans are for us tonight.

I am nervous and excited. I'm glad that I'll finally have been with all four men, but at the same time, my track record hasn't been so great this far. Reece seemed to have had fun last night, and I appreciate the way he let me take control.

But Mark and Tristan obviously were disappointments to all involved. They were disappointed in my performance, and I was disappointed in their reaction. So... what are the chances that Eli will be any better?

I take my bath, get dressed in a nice sundress, and am about to settle in with my book when there's a knock at the door. Vienna is gone, returning my lunch tray to the kitchen, so I'll have to get the door myself.

I pull the door open and see Eli standing there, a big grin on his face. "Hi?" It's a question when it comes out of my mouth. I'm not expecting him this early.

"Hey, Rose," he says, his hands clasped in front of him. "Uh... I was wondering if you might want to go down to the lake with me. I was thinking we could do a little fishing, and then... see what happens next."

I arch an eyebrow at him. "Fishing?"

He nods. "That's right."

In my experience, most shifters tend to fish in their wolf form because it's more fun that way, but I don't know if that's the case in every pack or just mine.

"Like... with a rod?"

"Uh-huh," he says, still smiling.

I'm not sure how I feel about this. I've never done it before. "Well... I don't have a rod," I tell him.

"That's okay. You can use my rod anytime." My eyebrows furrow as I stare at him, and his face turns a shade of red fairly similar to his hair.

"That's not what I... I mean... you can... but my fishing rod. You can... you can use that, too. I have a couple. You can borrow one. You can borrow my rod. My fishing rod!"

I try not to burst into laughter. I don't want to hurt his feelings. "Okay," I say. "What should I wear?"

"You can wear that," he says. "You look beautiful."

"Thank you," I tell him. "All right.... What do I need to bring?"

"Just yourself," he assures me.

I take a glance around the room and decide I'm ready to go. We walk down the hall to his room where he grabs a couple of fishing poles and a box of some kind. I know nothing about fishing. I volunteer to carry something, but he insists that he has it under control.

We walk out a door I've never gone through before and then down to the lake, which isn't too far away from the palace. It's beautiful, crystal clear, with lots of trees around it, and ducks floating by. It's a good size, too, with coves that go off in one direction or another, tucked behind the trees.

"I thought we could go over there," he says, pointing to a little secluded inlet. It takes a while to walk all the way around the lake to get there, but when we arrive, I see that we can get right down to the water, and there are some large rocks to sit on. Mature willow trees guard the area.

No one will even know we are down here unless they walk the long way around, as we have just done.

I discover that the box has some tackle in it but also drinks, snacks, and a couple of towels. I have to wonder why he brought those. Maybe he wants to sit on them?

"Have you ever fished before?" he asks me.

"No, not really," I reply as I watch him ready his fishing pole. "A few times, I've gone with some people from school who were fishing as wolves, but... I just kind of watched."

"Well, this is a lot more relaxing than that," he tells me. "I know wolves like to fish for sport, but we're not bears, after all."

We sit down on the rocks, and he hands me that first pole. He shows me how to cast, but I have no idea what I'm doing. I tell him, "I just hope I don't break your rod."

He chuckles, and I realize what I've said. "I am pretty sure you can't break it." Then, he leans over to me and says, "You know, I don't let just any woman touch my rod."

I feel myself blushing and can't help but giggle. Eli is funny. The other guys are all so serious, but he knows how to joke around, and I like that.

He casts his own line into the lake, and then we sit... and wait. I have no idea why people think this is fun. I would be bored if Eli wasn't so much fun to talk to.

We converse about his family, and he tells me some silly stories about adventures he and Kelly had when they were younger. It's nice to hear about my new friend and see her through the loving eyes of her brother.

"Hey, you've got a bite!" Eli exclaims, right in the middle of one of his stories. I don't know what he means. A bug bite? Another love bite?

He puts his own rod down and grabs a hold of mine, and I realize he's trying to tell me a fish is interested in what I'm offering.

"Take your time and bring it in nice and slowly." His large hand covers mine, and we slowly wind the line in… and eventually, I see a golden yellow fish flopping around on the surface of the water.

"Wow!" I shout to him. "Look at that!"

"That's a beauty," he tells me. "A sunfish!"

It is beautiful, but I feel bad. "Can we let it go?" I ask him. "Will it be hurt too badly to swim away?"

He looks at me for a second, and then a soft smile overtakes his face. "We can let it go," he says. "It'll be fine."

Eli finishes bringing it in and then somehow unhooks it from the lure before he tosses it back into the water.

"Bye, little fishy!" I shout. "Swim away!"

He chuckles and then looks over at me, catching my eyes, and I see a seriousness settles in.

Eli leans over and cups my face, and even though he smells a little fishy now, I want to kiss him, so when he presses his lips to mine, I lean into him.

The rods and other fishing apparatuses are forgotten as we continue to kiss, our hands exploring one another's bodies. His mouth settles on my neck, and I find myself gasping a little.

"The water is nice and warm," he says to me, a whisper near my ear. "Do you want to… take a dip?"

I stare at him for a moment. "I didn't bring my suit," I remind him.

He shrugs. "I don't think you'll need it. There's no one around."

I realize then what he is saying. He wants to go skinny dipping in the lake–and probably introduce me to his other rod.

We've been having such a good time, and I am looking forward to being with him, but I am nervous about someone seeing us.

"Don't worry, Rose," he tells me. "I'll keep you safe."

I find myself nodding, despite my reservations, and then, Eli is removing my shoes, untying my dress, and helping me step out of it. He kisses me gently as I slip my panties off, and then makes short work of undressing himself.

Though I feel odd sitting on this rock by the lake naked, I want him to get in first. He slides into the water and says, "It feels like a warm bath!"

"How deep is it?" I ask him.

"Oh, I'm guessing it's deep enough to fit my whole rod," he says, and my eyes bug before he starts laughing. "The water isn't that deep, sweetie. Come on in."

Sweetie? Is that going to be Eli's nickname for me?

He offers me his hand, and I take it, slipping into the water. He's right. It's warm, and my feet touch the bottom, a sandy surface, and the water completely covers my breasts.

And so do Eli's hands. He begins to gently rub my nipples as he kisses me, over and over again. He isn't wasting any time, though. Perhaps he thinks I might change my mind and get out before he gets to finish.

Eli lifts me up, my legs circling his waist, and he backs me up against the rocks we'd been sitting on earlier. He uses his fingers to make sure I am ready for him, and then he pushes inside of me.

The new element of the water makes everything feel different as he rams into me, time and time again. I steady myself with my arms on his shoulders, closing my eyes and concentrating on how good he feels. The water splashes around us, and I feel myself beginning to be carried away on waves of ecstasy.

When he tightens up beneath me and begins to grunt, I rest my head on his shoulder and wait for him to fill me with his seed. I wonder how to keep it inside of me when we are in the water, but I can't worry about that. If Eli isn't concerned, I shouldn't be either.

When we are done, I start to lower my feet back down to the bottom of the lake, but he holds me in place.

"Thank you, sweetie," he says. "That was amazing."

"Thank you for... letting me experience your rod," I reply.

He begins to laugh, and I think this is perfect. We end just like we started–laughing. The other guys might all be super serious, but Eli is fun, and I need more of that in my life right now.

CHAPTER 27: I'M SO STUPID

Eli

Her hand feels warm, clasped in my cool one, as we walk back to the castle.

"So, will we…. Tonight are we…." She doesn't have to finish her question for me to get what she is trying to ask.

"You want to see me again tonight?" I can see a pink color creep into her cheeks. Her question does echo my own thoughts. After already having had my turn with her at the lake, would going to her room tonight be so wrong? After all, tonight was still mine to spend with her.

"I was just wondering since we already… if tonight you would be with me again. After all, I was supposed to spend tonight with you," Rose remarks.

I nod slowly. I understand her sentiments totally, but sleeping with her again tonight would be having my go with her twice. That is not the agreement we had for this whole setup. Of course, I would jump at any chance of being with her again and again, but I have to consider the feelings of my fellow Alphas.

"I think you should rest tonight. As much as I would love to spend the night with you, I can promise that there will be no sleep happening if that were to be the case. I don't think I would be able to keep my hands off you." She smiles warmly at me, and the pink color in her cheeks gets more radiant. I wonder if she realizes how absolutely stunning she is.

Once we get inside, I walk her to her room. When we get to her door, she looks up at me with shimmering eyes. This woman has the most hypnotic eyes I have ever seen.

"Go rest now. I can't wait for the next time you get to play with my rod." At this, she giggles and I lean down to claim her lips. What I had meant to be a short parting kiss lingers as she draws me in when she parts her lips to accommodate mine.

I swirl my tongue in her mouth, tasting and feeling. A small moan comes from somewhere deep within her, and I find my hands reaching down. Cupping her buttocks, I draw her closer to me as I continue exploring the softer parts of her mouth.

I have to break this kiss before I open the door to her room where we can get some privacy while I take her one more time. Even though I had done so just a few hours ago, I still crave her. I don't think I can get enough of her; she is a temptation I definitely can't fight.

Softly I move back. I am trying to slow my breathing, and I can tell she is struggling as well.

"Bye," I whisper.

She wriggles her bottom lip and nods. I watch her enter her room, and I turn around. I feel bad walking away as I miss her already, but I know this might be a problem for the others. Discord is bound to happen with the other Alphas if they were to find out I'd had at her twice in the same day, and that would not be good for any of us, including Rose.

I can hear voices coming from my room, which leads me to the other Alphas. I wonder how their day went after we finished our basketball game and I left them. An uneasy hush falls upon the room when I walk in. I don't need a faith healer to feel the uneasiness in the room.

"Eli, nice of you to join us. I thought you were still busy with Rose down by the lake," Mark says. I can feel warmth in my face. I was very sure my little escapade had gone unnoticed, but it seems I've been wrong.

"We went fishing, but we are back now," I say plainly, trying to downplay the events of the day.

A shadow passes over Mark's face at my response. I know he knows more than he is letting on. I wonder why I am feeling like I have entered a judgment arena. What was so wrong with taking Rose out? If I hadn't, she would have spent the whole day alone in her room, probably bored.

"So, all you did was fish?" This time Tristan asks the question.

I swallow. Why am I suddenly being ganged up on? "No. I mean we…. we enjoyed each other's company."

"You had sex with her at the lake, didn't you?" Mark throws in. His question sounds more like a statement than a question.

"Yeah," I answer. I don't feel the need to hide the fact at this point. Today was my day with her. They had each gotten a chance to be with her already; what was so wrong with me having my turn?

"You had sex with Rose at the lake?" Reece asks in hushed sternness.

I can't help but roll my eyes at this point. Hadn't I already answered that question? What was their problem? "Yes. I took Rose out to the lake. And point of correction: I didn't have sex with her, I made love to her. Is that not what we are supposed to do to get her pregnant?"

Reece scoffs, and my eyes go to him. "You made love to her at the lake."

I gaze at him in silence, wondering if he wants me to answer or if that was also just a statement.

"Man, you can't be taking her to the lake for sex," Tristan chides.

I turn my gaze to him. I am confused now. "Did I not follow the schedule correctly? Wasn't today my turn?" I catch a glimpse of Mark shaking his head.

"Yeah, but we all did it properly. We didn't take a trip just to have sex with her. We waited for night to arrive and did our duty in the privacy of our rooms."

This time I laugh out loud. I think I am beginning to understand what is going on here.

"I was spontaneous. I wanted her to experience something fun and different. What is so wrong with that? As much as you all keep referring to this as a duty, you know we all view Rose as more than that—an object to accept our seed and subsequently carry our child. If she was only that, you wouldn't care where or how I took her." None of them say anything. I know I have spoken the truth.

"You won't charm yourself out of this one, mate. You went against the rules," Mark spits.

"When you took Rose out to the garden and kissed her, was that going against rules? What rules are we talking about here?" I push back.

Mark inhales and exhales at my statement. Of course, he didn't know that I had seen them in the garden during his night.

"Yeah, but that was me trying to make sure she was comfortable before our first night," Mark reasons and I smirk at him. He jerks his head back as though wondering why his answer had given me a reason to smile.

"Why would you want to make sure she is comfortable? It's just a duty, right?" I interrogate.

Again there is silence, although the tension I had sensed earlier seems to be evaporating.

"You make us look bad. I mean you are busy taking her on a rendezvous and fishing. Why not just do what we all did?" Reece presses.

"Huh, there it is. You are all worried about being outshined by me, but that's because you all have formed a bond with Rose. A bond way deeper than just a duty. Hell, I won't deny what I feel for Rose. To me, she is not just my duty. I want to make her happy."

I can hear mumbling amongst them.

"So you would be okay with me taking her out to a romantic dinner on a rooftop somewhere?" Reece asks.

I chuckle. "If you plan to wine and dine her and not throw her off said rooftop, I'd be more than happy with that. Anything that keeps her smiling and happy is good enough for me. If you hurt her, then that will be a problem. If you make her cry, then I'll have a reason to fight you. I treasure Rose and want her to be happy at all costs. If we do that for her, then what's the problem?"

"Hmm, you have a weird take on things, don't you?" Tristan remarks.

"I just have a rational way of viewing things. As much as we are in a competition to impregnate her, we all have the same frame of mind to protect her at all costs. That's good enough for me."

Mark nods at my statement. I am not much of a mind reader, but I do hope they all follow my lead and stop pitting themselves against each other. Our main priority needs to be to make Rose comfortable and happy if we truly care about her like we say we do.

"So are you planning to go be with her again tonight?" Reece questions, and they all look at me with clear anticipation of my answer.

"We've all had a turn with her in succession, night after night. Tonight, the plan is, she soaks in a warm fragrant bath and rests. Too much of anything, even good, can become tiring. Our woman needs her beauty rest. Don't you agree?"

They all continue to stare at me. Calling her OUR woman is probably weird, even to my own mind, but that's the reality we all have to contend with.

She is our precious, sweet love, and us four noble Alphas need to protect her. I am willing to take part in this journey, however weird it is to share her. I just wonder if they are all cooperative enough to walk it with me in a way that satisfies our Rose.

CHAPTER 28: VISITING THE DOCTOR AGAIN

The feel of my arm entwined with Shelby's is comforting. We walk down the same passage we once walked when I first arrived here almost two months ago.

"Do I look pregnant? Are there any signs I need to be on the lookout for? I know a pregnant woman pukes… a lot. I haven't puked. Also, I read somewhere they pee often. How do I know if I am peeing a lot or have just been drinking too much of that pineapple juice? I read that pineapples can be harmful to pregnant women; do you think I should switch to mango juice instead?" I ask all these questions fast and in succession.

Shelby whistles. "Slow down, girlfriend. All this worrying is also not good for a baby, so chill. We'll soon find out if you are. I don't know if I can answer the load of questions you just piled on me. I'm not even sure if I remember all of them with you talking so fast."

I exhale and chuckle.

When I'm nervous, I do tend to talk fast. Sometimes, I end up tripping over my own words. I'm wondering what the doctor is going to say. I am nervous. I want to be pregnant, but I'm also afraid that if I am pregnant, then that would mean the end of my time with the

Alphas, and that would mean the end of my duties here is getting closer. After having the baby, that would be it.

Wait, if I'm not pregnant despite my magical uterus, will the king replace me? Would it mean that I've failed? I've done everything I could have.

After each time I spent with an Alpha, I would lay on my back and look like a fool with my legs up… except for that one time with Eli. I'm sure his seed was washed away by the lake water. I hope a fish doesn't end up ingesting his sperm. Was that even possible? I doubt it, but I could picture a little fish hybrid with gorgeous red hair. Aquawolf… I need to stop watching those sci-fi films. I'm having crazy thoughts. I'm not sure how everything works. Could one get pregnant if they had sex in water though?

I want to ask Shelby, but I know she will just tell me to calm down again. I can't help but bite down hard on my lips. The little pain that it causes is enough to take my mind off everything, if only for a little while.

Shelby brings up her other hand and squeezes my arm. Sometimes I feel like she can read my mind as she always senses when I am worrying or not all right. I'm grateful to have her here with me right now, supporting me. I've known her for just two months, but already I feel like she has become more than just a friend to me. She is my confidant and sister. I feel so close to her, and if I were to leave this place, I would miss her so much.

"You'll be fine," she reassures as her eyes meet mine.

I smile at her, and she returns the gesture. I think I love her… is it allowed to love another woman? I don't feel like I would want to spend a night with her or anything…. Neither would I want her watching me as I bathe again, but I have come to care deeply for her.

A wave of disinfectant floods my nostrils when we walk into the doctor's office. I smile and breathe a sigh of relief when my eyes land on the smiling face of Nurse Nancy, who is seated behind the counter.

"Hello," she greets us with an air of welcome. Her cheery voice kind of undoes the knots of anxiety that were gripping me.

"Good morning, Nurse Nancy," we say in unison.

Nurse Nancy directs us to sit in some chairs on the left side of the room. I keep fidgeting as we wait for her to come and attend to us. I am so nervous; I am struggling to take much-needed oxygen into my lungs. Shelby keeps patting my arm reassuringly, but I can't help the surge of nausea and lightheadedness I am suddenly feeling.

Wait? Weren't these pregnancy symptoms?

"Take this little cup and please go fill it with your urine in the bathroom over there." Nurse Nancy is standing in front of us and talking. She points to a door at the far end of the room.

I swallow hard and nod as I accept the little cup she hands me. I leave Shelby sitting and make my way to the bathroom, my legs like jelly.

After managing to fill the cup with my urine, I wash my hands while I look at my reflection in the bathroom mirror. I'm amazed that I had any urine since Vienna had been instructed to make sure I drank nothing when I woke up. She had said something about not diluting the specimen. Whatever that meant.

A lump has formed in my throat, and I feel like I'm going to puke. I pick up the little cup and make my way back to the waiting room.

Nurse Nancy takes the cup and asks me to go into the inner examination room, saying that the doctor would be there with me soon. Again I find myself on the bed with my thighs splayed open and feet in stirrups. Wasn't there another way to do these exams?

Well, I will try to look as pretty as I can for the doctor. As I wait for her, I find myself trying to think back to what the doctor's name was again. Doctor Poltergeist? No, that doesn't sound right. I squint my eyes at the bright light shining above me. Doctor Pentecost? I shake my head again. Why was I finding it hard to remember her name?

When the doctor comes in a few minutes later, she's with Nurse Nancy and Shelby. Ah, did Shelby really have to be in here to see me like this? Well, I could use some moral support though.

'Dr. Pendergan,' I silently read the name printed on her lab coat. Ah, so I wasn't too far off with her name. I had the 'P' right.

Shelby smiles at me as if she's trying to transfer comfort to me through the tilt of her lips. I manage a tired smile back.

I try to prepare myself as much as possible for the internal exam I know is coming.

"Hello honey, I hope you are all right," the doctor greets me as she smiles.

"Good morning, Dr. Pendergan. I am well and you?"

"I'm great, honey. Now I'll just do the same little examination we did the last time. Just relax," she gently demands.

Relaxing is easier said than done, but before I know it, she's removing her gloves and the exam is over. Well, that wasn't so bad. She takes a chart that Nurse Nancy hands to her.

Before she talks, Shelby raises a hand. "Give us the dumbed-down version, Doctor," she says. I know how doctors like using the medical jargon, and personally, I'd have let her amuse herself, but Shelby wasn't shy about asking for what she wanted.

I'm too nervous and scared of her verdict.

The scowl on her face shows she's not pleased by Shelby's interruption, but soon she's back to smiling again.

"Everything looks okay. You are in good health and at your peak, but you are not pregnant yet."

I look up at Shelby. How was that for the dumbed-down version? I had failed to get pregnant. My uterus is not as magical as they assumed. Four strong Alphas and none of their seed has been accepted by my eggs. Maybe my eggs are just as stubborn as I am. Or maybe they are a bit lost on what to do with the seed. I assume my eggs are as inexperienced in these matters as I am.

I shake my head. Why am I acting like my uterus and eggs have a conscience of some kind?

The doctor smiles encouragingly, but I'm too distraught by the news to smile back this time.

"So what do I do? Tell me, doctor. How can I improve my chances of getting pregnant? I'll do anything."

She shakes her head. "You have to keep trying, honey. It would have been quite a miracle if you had gotten pregnant within the first month. Because of the uniqueness of your womb, it appears you ovulate twice each month. This means your chances of getting pregnant fast are very high. Pray to the Moon Goddess, and soon it will happen. Don't dwell too much on it. Stress produces hormones that are not conducive for conceiving, so relax."

Shelby clears her throat rather too loudly. I know this is her way of saying, 'I told you so.'

I feel sad that I'm not pregnant yet, but also glad as this means I get to spend more time with the Alphas. This might be a blessing in disguise. The Alphas are all different in their own ways, but they all bring their unique flavors to my table. Oh, how I relish in all they have to dish out for me, and I crave more.

This means I get to spend more time with each of them. My Alphas…. Yes, that sounded right. At least for now, they all belong to big-nosed and double-horned uterus breeder me.

Take that, Emily.

CHAPTER 29: WINNING

Mark

All four of us were unsettled at breakfast, knowing today is the day that Rose will be going to the doctor to discover whether or not she is pregnant. It is my turn to be with her, assuming she isn't pregnant, so part of me is hopeful that it hasn't happened yet.

That seems silly. I should be hoping that she is pregnant and that the baby is mine so that I can be the king, but I see so many downsides to having it be my child she's carrying that I'm honestly not sure how I feel about it.

After all, the "winner" has to marry Emily, and I know I don't want to do that. I'm not sure which is worse–not getting to be king or having to marry that crazy bitch.

Rather than going into my room to work or do something fun, I am pacing the hallway near Rose's room. I'm a bit surprised I am the only Alpha out here, but maybe the others are not as on edge as I am to find out what the situation is.

When I see Rose and Shelby coming down the hallway, I stare at them, digging my toes into the bottoms of my shoes to try to keep from running over to her. I want to go and ask Rose what the doctor said, but I wait as patiently as I can for her to grow closer.

"Alpha Mark?" she asks, her forehead creased. "What are you doing here?"

"Hi, Rose," I say. "I just… wanted to see how it went and make sure you're okay."

Rose opens her mouth to answer me, but it's Shelby who interjects, "As if you care!"

I turn and glare at her, but Rose puts a hand on her arm. "I'm fine, Mark, thank you." Rose plasters a smile to her face, but I don't quite believe her. I think something is wrong.

"Did the doctor–"

Before I can finish my question, Eli's door opens, and the other three Alphas come out. "Hey, Mark," Eli calls, "King Gene wants to see us." He notices Rose, and a grin forms on his face.

The other two are smiling at her, too. Eli greets her. "Hello, Rose, sweetie."

She lifts a hand and waves at him, and I notice her cheeks turn pink. "Hello, Eli. Reece, Tristan," she says, though the way she says Tristan's name isn't as friendly.

"Hello, darlin'," Reece says while Tristan replies, "Good morning, my little flower."

Does everyone have a nickname for her?

"Come on," Reece says to me, and I know I have to go because it's the king, after all.

"I'll be back," I tell her, and she sort of shrugs. She really is angry with me still, after all these weeks.

The four of us go to visit the king, who only wants to see us to tell us that Rose is not pregnant yet, something she would've told me herself if he'd given me two seconds. He also says that the physician thinks it's best that we keep trying because of her unique two uterine horn anatomy. Something seems slightly off about King Gene, almost like he's happy that she's not pregnant, which seems odd to me, but I can't question it at the moment. I'm too excited.

Since she's not pregnant, that makes tonight my night with Rose.

I head back to the hall where our rooms are ahead of everyone else, not wanting to hear the other guys talk about the rules or what

I'm supposed to do. I'm so sick of all of this squabbling, and I am beginning to realize that if Rose starts to have feelings for more than one of us, we will have to figure out a way to get along.

After all, her happiness is more important than our egos.

I knock on her door and wait for her to call me in, but her maid pulls it open, her eyebrows raised. "Yes?"

"May I speak to Rose, please?" I ask her.

The maid looks over her shoulder, and a moment later, Rose is there, pulling the door open wider.

"Hi, baby," I say, smiling timidly at her. She swallows hard, and I know I've got a lot of convincing to do. "Can I come in?"

She purses her lips, pulling them to one side of her face before she nods, and I enter.

"Vienna, you can go," she pardons her maid, and Vienna gives me a narrowed glance before she walks out the door.

Rose walks over to a chair by the window, and I sit on the windowsill next to her. "What is it, Mark?" she asks. "If you're here to tell me you want to forgo your turn because the first time was so miserable… I'll understand."

"Miserable?" I repeat. "Rose, you have to know I would never say anything like that. That was all Emily."

She looks at me for a moment, but I can see she doesn't believe me.

I drop to my knees and reach for her hands. "Baby, I had the best time of my life with you. There's no one I'd rather be with. Anywhere. Believe me, if I didn't mean it, I would just haul my ass in here later and get through it. But you are more important to me than this stupid contest."

Her eyes widen. "You can't mean that. The throne–"

"The throne is nothing if you're upset with me, baby." I mean it, and I hope she can see it in my eyes.

A tear forms in the corner of her left eye, and as it spills over, I reach over and wipe it away with my thumb.

I can't wait to be with her again. I don't want to wait until the sun goes down–I want her now.

I lean in and find her lips, kissing her softly, and she hesitates but then reaches for me, her soft hands resting on either side of my face.

She leans forward, and I deepen the kiss, wrapping my arms around her and pulling her toward me. I move so that I'm between her legs, and I can't help but sift my hands through her hair, breathing in her cantaloupe scent.

She makes a soft moaning noise, and I whisper to her, "Rose, I want you now."

Her breath catches in her lungs as she pulls back slightly and looks at me, still cupping my face. She nods, and then I know that she's forgiven me for what she thought I'd said.

Scooping her up, I move her to the bed, depositing her in the middle as she kicks off her sandals. I fall on top of her, continuing to kiss her as I slowly undress her, taking my time and rubbing my hands all over her.

She pulls my shirt off over my head and fumbles with the button and zipper on my jeans as I discard my shoes and socks. In my boxers, I slide down the length of her beautiful, naked body, and spread her legs, hoping to give her some more pleasure this time before I get my own.

I run my tongue up the length of her and then between each of her folds, probing her as deep as I can, tasting her, and then taking her nub between my lips and sucking her gently until she begins to rock her hips, her fingers woven through my hair. When she cries out, and I feel her go into spasm around my face, I know my job is done.

I kiss her soft mound before I stand up and strip out of my underwear, reclaiming my place between her slick thighs.

Smiling down at her, I notice her slitted eyes and the sheen of perspiration on her fair skin. I press inside of her, glad it no longer hurts her like it did the first time, and then, I slowly begin to move my hips, thrusting gently at first and then picking up speed. Her fingertips run the length of me, and though I manage to get her back to her peak and keep her there for a few moments, she feels so good, I can't last as long as I'd like to.

I deposit my specimen as deeply inside her as possible and hope that those little suckers will swim as fast as they can up the right path to the uterine horn that's discharging this time, but at the same time, I'm just happy to be with her.

Completely spent, I roll off her and pull her to my chest, grabbing a blanket and tossing it over us. "Thank you so much, baby," I tell her.

Her eyes are still half-closed as she lays her head on my chest. "You're amazing," she whispers. "Especially with your tongue. Well, and your… and other parts of you."

I snicker and brush her hair back. "Thank you," I repeat. "You're pretty damn amazing yourself."

"Nah," she denies. "I just lay here."

"You inspire me with your beautiful body," I confess.

She wrinkles her nose up at me, like she disagrees.

"What?" I ask her. "Surely, you know you're beautiful."

Rose shrugs. "I have never felt beautiful. My parents always told me I was average looking so I shouldn't expect too much."

My eyebrows arch, and I find myself saying, "Oh, I didn't realize your parents were sightless."

"What?" she asks, her forehead crinkling.

"Well, they must be to say something like that."

"No, they're not."

"Are they just stupid then?" I question.

She laughs. "No… well, I mean, they're not very nice, but no one back home ever said I was even pretty, so–"

"So your entire pack is full of stupid people who can't see very well. Got it."

Another giggle escapes her lips. "I don't think so."

"Well, I know that you're gorgeous, so that's the only explanation."

Shaking her head, she explains, "My nose is too long for my face, for one thing."

"This nose?" I slide my finger down her nose before I lean down and kiss the tip of it. "You have a perfect nose, Rose."

"Thanks," she accepts, "but even Emily pointed it out the first time she saw me."

"Emily is an idiot," I tell her. "Believe me, I've seen girls with big noses before." I think of that maid from the breakfast room. "You do not have one."

She smiles at me. "You're too sweet."

"I'm just being honest. So… your parents aren't very nice. What about siblings?"

"It's just me," she explains. "I never had a lot of friends either. Everyone was always afraid to get too close to me because my father was the Alpha. They thought I was too good for them. Even though I had to work jobs in other packs, like at a sewage treatment facility."

"Really?" I ask her, my eyes widening.

She nods. "Yeah, gross, huh?"

"I couldn't do that," I admit. "But I admire you for doing what needed to be done to help your family."

She takes a deep breath in and looks away, and I think there's something she's not telling me. But she asks me a question before I can clarify. "What about you? Tell me about your family."

"Oh, well, that's a long story. Basically, my dad is a perfectionist who always expected me to do everything exactly as he would, and when I'd fail, he'd be the first to tell me. He stepped down about ten years ago, and he and his second mate are living on the beach while I run the kingdom, and my little brother spends all of the money my dad saved up over his career."

"Seriously?" she interjects, and it is my turn to shrug.

"At least he's not spending pack money," I declare. "It's fine, though. If I become king, that'll show my father that he was wrong about me."

Rose reaches up and touches my face, and I realize I feel comfortable bearing my soul to her.

"This isn't just a competition to you, though," she realizes quietly.

"No, it's not a competition at all," I admit. "Rose, I care more about you than I do winning this contest or the throne. I just want to be with you. You make me happy."

She smiles and lifts her lips to mine in a sweet kiss, and I feel like I could tell her anything, and she would make me feel better about it, no matter how traumatic.

Rose is amazing, and she is the real prize here, not the kingdom. Not to me, anyway.

CHAPTER 30: IT'S ALL ABOUT EMILY

EMILY

I march through the lengthy corridors, escorted by my entire entourage .Pausing for a moment in front of one of the enormous mirrors adorning the walls, I take a moment to admire myself while also making sure I project a strong presence inside these confines; after all, I am the future Luna.

A tall woman stares back at me in the reflection, her long hair pulled up into a flawless and exquisite bun on top of her head, her face proudly displayed.

Arrogantly admiring herself, the reflection glances down her exquisite nose. Her pale skin looks stunning with dark red lipstick. I can't help but smile when I see myself in the mirror; I am the epitome of a Luna.

My gaze wanders over my form; I'm dressed in a pricey spider silk gown that fits my curves and accentuates my best features. The top is jet black and has a low cut, displaying the top of my undoubtedly magnificent chest, which is the focal point of the garment.

I reach out to touch the jewelry that hangs around my neck. I can't help but smile as a huge red ruby dangles just above my cleavage.

With such a large stone, I'm confident that I'll be able to steer attention to exactly where I want it.

I enjoy being the focus of attention. No man can help but gaze in my direction; if they don't, they're either blind, stupid, or both. It always amuses me to watch them drool on themselves over me.

The dress falls to my generous hips, flares out, and turns crimson red. The gown has a slit on the right side that nearly reaches my hip, displaying a long stretch of my strong and gorgeous legs.

Numerous little gems are sewn throughout the dress, and they sparkle in the light and glimmer when I move. On my feet, I'm wearing a pair of red heels that add a couple of inches to my height, which is ideal for my future Alpha's huge frame.

I'm definitely built perfectly for one of those handsome hunks, not the stupid breeder girl.

I do hope she leaves soon as her presence is just becoming an annoyance now. I mean, do we really need a breeder? If I can just seduce one of the Alphas and get pregnant before she does, would there be a need for some stupid competition and her unwanted presence?

I'm not even sure that I'm willing to raise any offspring she bears… it might actually have that Pinocchio nose of hers. Who wants that?

What I'm wearing might be a bit of an overkill just to go for an afternoon walk in the garden with hopes that I might just 'run' into one of the Alphas. Whichever one of them I run into will definitely not be able to resist me looking like this.

I can't help but hum in satisfaction as I admire pure perfection. I turn to my lady in waiting; I need some validation. "Do I not look beautiful, Tara?"

Tara, who stands off to my right, nods dutifully and in a complimentary voice says, "Yes, mistress. As always, you can capture the attention of an entire room."

"Yes, I surely can," I purr in agreement. I am definitely a catch. Now, I just need to find a way to run into one of the Alphas. It's time they got to see the true definition of a woman and not keep drooling over some dirty breeder who doesn't even know how to color match her outfits.

I mean who wears sundress like the one she has on today? It's got so many colors one would swear a unicorn got drunk and puked all the colors of the rainbow onto her.

Turning from the mirror, I make my way to the dining room where I hope the Alphas are gathered.

I pass a few servants along the way who stare at me. I bet they can't believe I am real. I'm definitely out of this world in terms of looks and style.

One of the maids, who is dusting a statue in the foyer, frowns as I pass her. Jealous much? I know every woman wants to be me, but there can only be one queen, Luna Emily.

The dining room is empty except for some servants who are polishing the silverware. They too stop and stare. Maybe if they took a picture it would last longer. Have they really never seen a beautiful woman before? Well, I guess I can't exactly blame them; I am, after all, one of a kind.

I proceed to walk toward the door that leads into the manicured gardens on the left wing of the castle. Before I can reach the door, a tall shadow is cast as a broad-shouldered man makes his way inside. Bingo!

"Oh, Alpha Reece. Fancy running into you here. My retinue was just accompanying me to take a walk in the garden. Would you like to join me?"

I can see his eyes widen as he takes in my full form. Wonderful! This is exactly what I wanted. I raise my hands to cup and adjust my breasts, just another trick I have mastered to bring his attention to them.

When I look at him, I realize his eyes are focusing on my shoes. Oh, was the big boy shy? He can't look at my breasts or my face. I find that charming.

He coughs a little before clearing his throat. "Are you planning to take a walk in the gardens in those shoes?"

What? Was that all he had to say? Could he not see the rest of me?

"Ahh, I'm quite used to dressing with such finesse, even if it is just for a short walk. That is how PROPER ladies conduct themselves. We never need a special occasion to look good," I say as I wave my arms, causing my bangles to jingle noisily.

"I see." His tone is cool and indifferent as he brings his eyes up to regard my face. His brows come together as he looks at me.

I can't help but wonder what he is thinking. Can't he see me? I mean, like really see me?

I stand up a bit straighter, making sure to bring my leg forward a bit, to show off my exposed flesh through the slit. I arch my back slightly just to make my breasts more prominent. He will definitely see me now.

"So, will you be a gentleman and accompany me on my walk?" I ask in a high-pitched voice. I have to sound a bit more feminine. Men love that.

He puts his hands into his pockets and again clears his throat. Was he catching a cold or something? I smile, however, at the move to put his hands in his pockets. I am sure he is trying to hide the bulge that must be forming in his pants. Emily has a way of causing men to go gaga.

"I am… I have a thing… I have to go do some work… I have a lot of urgent paperwork I need to see to. Yes, paperwork. Rain check?"

I can't help but chuckle at his stutter. Well, my beauty tends to render men speechless. I walk toward him now and stand a few inches away from him. I bring my hand up, and using my long fingernail, trail the width of his chest.

"Aww, can't that wait? I would really love to spend some quality time with you." I wink at him suggestively and lick my lips for emphasis.

He steps back, looking a bit restless. Why is he playing hard to get? I'm offering all of this to him on a silver platter. Why doesn't he just take it?

I take another step toward him. I am determined to get him. Maybe he is afraid of the repercussions of taking me without the king's say. I need to reassure him that it's okay.

"The paperwork really can't wait. Every second I delay getting to work is damaging to my pack. I'm sorry. Maybe another time."

This time I swing my arms around his neck and lean my breasts into his chest. His face is a few inches away from mine, and I can feel his breath caressing my cheeks.

"A few minutes is all I ask for, bae," I whisper as I lean closer to his ear.

He doesn't move. His hands remain in his pockets.

"With all due respect, Emily, please get your hands off me. I am not interested in whatever you are offering. Wait for whoever will be king and your husband to do… all this."

I am offended but don't move back. "Well, that person could be you, cutie pie. I mean, if you were to impregnate me as Luna, my cousin would have no choice but to cancel this whole nonsense. You would be declared the winner by default." I dangle the prospect of winning in front of him. I bet he can't resist now.

Suddenly, his gaze moves up, and he looks past me. I can't see what he is looking at, but I catch a faint whiff of sweat coming from him. He removes his hands from his pockets and encircles my waist. Well, that was easy enough. Just when I think he is embracing me, he lifts me slightly and pushes me to the side.

"Rose, darlin', wait!" he calls out and takes off before I can say anything more. I turn around in time to see him chasing after the retreating back of the woman I recognize as the dirty breeder.

Wait, had he just left me for that—that thing? He is running after her, and leaving Emily?

This has to be some twisted nightmare I am having. This can't be real. What is going on here? And did he just call that filth da–darlin'?

End of Book 1

Mated With Four Alphas: Pregnant With Four Alphas' Babies Book 2
Chapter 1 is included with your purchase!

Bella Moondragon
and
Olivia Bhelle Kildare
Mated With Four Alphas
Pregnant With Four Alphas' Babies
Book 2

MATED WITH FOUR ALPHAS
CHAPTER 1: SLUMBER PARTY
WITH TRISTAN

Rose

Seeing Reece in the garden with Emily was unsettling, to say the least, and I didn't give him a chance to explain. I couldn't just stand there and listen to him try to tell me it wasn't what it looked like.

Unless he wasn't planning on saying anything like that at all.

I rush back to my room, trying to remember that I'm supposed to be focusing on Tristan today, not Reece. I'll have to worry about him tomorrow.

Somehow, before I get to my door, Reece appears in the hallway in front of me, out of breath.

"Rose!" he says, stopping and doubling over. "Wait."

I stare at him, look down the hallway in the other direction, where he came from, and then back at him. "How did you get here so fast?" I ask him.

"The other door…." He is still breathing hard, but he takes a few steps toward me now. "Listen, Emily was coming on to me, but I was telling her no. My hands were in my pockets. I just… didn't want you to think that anything had happened between us. Because nothing did."

I can tell that he means it, but my heart is still rattled. "Okay," I finally manage.

"Seriously–you believe me, right?"

I nod. "Sure." At the moment, I don't know what to think, but I do know I don't want him to worry about it while I try to sort it out.

"Oh, thank you, little darlin'," he says, moving over to me. He wraps his arms around me and pulls me close. With my cheek pressed against his muscular chest, I can't help but feel like everything is all right, and I shouldn't be too concerned.

He clearly has feelings for me.

But then... whoever wins will end up with Emily anyway, so maybe he should be getting to know her better.

Just in case.

It's not as if any of these men actually belong to me.

In Reece's arms, though, I feel like he is mine, or at least like he is more mine than he is hers.

"Thank you, Rose," he says again before he kisses my cheek. "I want to kiss you on the lips, but I guess I'll have to wait until tomorrow for that. I don't want anyone to accuse me of trying to take more time than I'm allotted."

I nod–the rules to this contest are growing more complex every day.

Later that afternoon, I receive a handwritten note from Tristan that says, "Little flower, your presence is requested at my room tonight at 9:00. Please wear your most comfortable pajamas, bring your toothbrush, a change of clothing, and anything that you need in order to spend the night as this will be a sleepover."

As I read over the note a second time, my face begins to turn a little pink.

Clearly, Tristan has learned his lesson from last time.

"What is it?" Vienna asks me. "Are you well, miss?"

"I'm fine," I tell her. "Just... Tristan's invitation is so sweet." I hand it to her, and she reads over it and then smiles.

"This could be fun," she says. "We should get you a teddy bear and a little blankie to take with you. You know, like when we were girls and used to have sleepovers at friends' houses."

I nod, but I didn't have a lot of friends from when I was younger, and then there was all the kicking I'd done so I don't really know firsthand what she's talking about when it comes to fun sleepovers, but I can imagine.

A few hours later, I am ready to go to Tristan's. Vienna is very resourceful and has found me an overnight duffle bag, a teddy bear, some cute pajamas that are nothing like the sexy ones I usually wear for my men, and has packed us some snacks, as well as my necessities.

When Tristan knocks on the door, I smile at him, my hair in pigtails as I am already wearing a onesie with different colored hearts all over it.

His eyes widen, and then he cracks into a grin. "Well, hello there," he says. "Don't you look adorable?"

I shrug. "I never really got to have a sleepover when I was younger, so I figured I may as well indulge myself in the fun of it all."

He laughs. "I'm glad to be the first one to have you over for such a fun event, then."

Tristan offers me his hand, and I take it. He leads me to his room where he changes out of his suit and into a pair of pajamas. I am surprised to see he has a grown-up version of superhero pajamas, with little symbols on the pants and a removable cape.

"Would you like to watch a movie?" he asks me. "That's what I used to do with my friends at sleepovers. We could play some video games, too, though I don't think we'll go wrap toilet paper around anyone's house."

"Did you do that?" I ask him, sitting on his bed and holding the new teddy bear Vienna found for me.

"Oh, yeah. TPing houses was great fun, but I can't imagine the king would think it was cool if we did that."

"Actually," I say, trying not to laugh. "Later tonight, we could go TP the other Alphas' doors. I'm not sure how to make it stick but–"

"Get it wet," he says with a shrug, and we both burst out laughing.

We get comfy on the bed and watch a funny movie while eating pizza, junk food, and popcorn instead of the formal meals we usually have. We drink way too much soda–though Tristan also has a beer or two–and then we play a video game that he is really good at. Me, not so much.

After that, he asks, "Do you want to watch a scary movie?" My eyebrows raise. "Oh, come on. I'll keep you safe."

I let out a deep breath and agree, and he puts in a movie I've never even heard of before about a possessed doll.

It is terrifying, and before it's even halfway over, I find myself with my head buried in his chest.

"You're safe, little flower," he says to me.

I look up into his eyes, and his mouth comes down on mine.

We begin to kiss as if it's the only thing that will save us from that devil doll. His hands roam over the soft fabric of my onesie, and then… he is unbuttoning it, and I couldn't care less about what's on the television.

Tristan completely unbuttons my pajamas, and I slip my arms out. Then, he pulls his shirt off over his head and takes off his pants, turning the television off before he climbs back into bed with me. We are naked, and he is touching me, his mouth devouring mine.

He pulls me close as his other hand settles between my legs. "You're so wet," he whispers against my lips.

I take his thick cock in my hand. "You're so hard," I remind him.

"Well, I guess there's just one thing to do about this."

He slides on top of me, and I spread my legs for him. With one quick thrust, he moves inside of me, and his pace increases quickly. I moan, a mix of pain and pleasure, and he all but stops, staring down at me.

"Sorry, little flower," he says in a gentle voice. "I'll be easier on you."

"I'm okay," I tell him, lovingly stroking his cheek.

He shakes his head. "I want to savor you."

Tristan starts moving his hips again, but this time, his pace is much slower, and with each movement of his hips, he grinds against me. It feels so good, I am putty beneath him in only a matter of moments. I wrap my arms around him and hold him tight.

It takes a long time for him to join me in my euphoria, but in that time, my mind has grown cloudy as my thoughts jumble together. Everything about the way he is touching me is heavenly, and when he finally comes, my body begins to tingle with electricity.

When he's finished, he holds me close, and I concentrate on the sensation of my body coming back to this plane. I feel like I've been in another dimension.

Pressed against his chest, I listen to his heartbeat as he gently caresses me. "Thank you, Rose, for being so amazing," he says. "That was… so special. I've never been with a woman like that before."

I smile at him and run my palm along his cheek, rough with unshaved whiskers. "You're welcome. Thank you," I tell him as he catches my hand and kisses it.

"You know, when I was younger, there was a woman who was a maid to my mother who was very beautiful. She was about fifteen years older than me, and she started working in our house when I was ten. She would always look at me in this certain way that made me think about women way before the rest of my friends even knew they existed… apart from their mothers and aunts. Anyway, Camilla waited until I was fifteen to make her move, and by then, I thought I was ready."

"She propositioned you when you were fifteen?" I ask him. When I was fifteen, I still thought babies came from a stork.

He nods. "Yeah, in a closet near my father's study. She said she was going to teach me how to be a man. And in some ways, I guess she did, but she wanted it rough…. And quick so we didn't get caught. I thought… I thought that's how it was supposed to go, you know? If she wasn't in pain, I wasn't doing it right." He drops his head and shakes it slowly.

"So that's how you've always been with all of the women you've slept with?" I ask him.

His eyes meet mine. "That's right. It never occurred to me that some women would rather just take it slow and enjoy it. With you… I get that."

I smile up at him. "Thank you for sharing that with me, Tristan. It means a lot to me."

"Thank you for being so easy to talk to," he replies. He leans down and kisses me, and I believe we have bonded on a new level.

We lie there together for about an hour, and I am just about to doze off when Tristan asks me, "So… are you ready?"

At first, I think he means to have sex again, but then I remember our secret mission. Laughing, I say, "Oh, I'm ready."

Both of us are chuckling like kids as we get dressed and go to the bathroom to find our secret weapon.

It's too bad I won't get to see the other Alphas' faces when they walk out of their rooms in the morning. Now, that would be funny!

Mated With Four Alphas: Pregnant With Four Alphas' Babies Book 2 can be found here.

Banter of the Devil

The Mafia Kings series

Indebted to the Mafia King

<u>Loved by the Mafia King</u>

Claimed by the Mafia King (releases 11/15/2024)

Sign up for Bella's newsletter here.

Follow Bella on Facebook here.